Rabbitmagic

Rabbitmagic

HOLLY WEBB

SCHOLASTIC INC.

New York   Toronto   London   Auckland
Sydney   Mexico City   New Delhi   Hong Kong

ISBN 978-0-545-16054-4

12 11 10 9 8 7 6 5 4 3 2 1   10 11 12 13 14 15/0

Printed in the U.S.A.   40
First U.S. edition, April 2010

For Jon, Tom, Robin, and William

1

Lottie walked slowly up the street, her dachshund, Sofie, held tightly in her arms, and Giles the hamster perched on her shoulder. Her best friend, Ruby, walked next to her, close enough that Lottie could hear her breathing. It was early on Sunday morning.

Lottie laughed to herself, hugging Sofie closer.

"What is it?" Ruby asked. She looked pale, but she seemed fine otherwise, Lottie thought, looking at her carefully. The spell that had been put on Ruby was definitely gone.

"Oh, I was just thinking . . . when Mum sent me to live here, I had no idea what it would be like. I was just angry that she'd dumped me on Uncle Jack. If you'd told me — what, four months ago? — that I'd be living in a shop full of magical animals, I'd never have believed you." Lottie shook her head wonderingly.

"Do you — do you wish you hadn't?" Ruby asked her slowly.

Lottie looked up sharply. "Of course not!" She felt Sofie's tense muscles shift with relief. Sofie was Lottie's familiar and they were learning magic together. But Sofie was never quite sure how much Lottie loved her, whether she would suddenly decide to go back to her mother and leave Sofie behind here in Netherbridge. "How could I?" Lottie asked. "There's Sofie, and you, and Uncle Jack, and Danny. And all the other animals in the shop. I wouldn't ever want to go back to how I was before. When animals didn't talk, and magic was just in fairy tales." Lottie shivered a little, rubbing her cheek against Sofie's velvet ear, and Sofie licked her lovingly. "It would be better if it was just the good bits of fairy tales, though. I'm not so keen on the evil enchantresses like Pandora. If you'd said we'd be going out on a Sunday morning to fight one of those, I'd have thought you were as crazy as Pandora is."

Lottie and Ruby looked at each other and grinned. Lottie had just survived doing the most impulsive thing she'd ever done. She still didn't know how. She and Sofie had walked willingly into a fight with a crazed witch. They'd had to. Pandora had had Ruby under a spell, stitched into an enchanted drawing, and it was the only way to save her. Lottie wasn't quite sure how they'd gotten out alive, let alone how they still had control over their own minds. She shook her head slowly. Everything still seemed to work.

They pushed open the door of Grace's Pet Shop, making the bell jangle cheerfully, and Uncle Jack looked around the door that led to the kitchen, holding a piece of peanut butter toast. "Oh, it's you lot. What are you doing up so early on a Sunday, girls? Want some toast?"

"Can we take it upstairs?" Lottie asked. She was going to have to explain where she'd been to Uncle Jack sometime soon, she knew, but she wanted to talk over everything that had happened with the others first.

Uncle Jack sliced huge slabs of bread and slid them under the broiler, and a couple of minutes later Lottie carried a teetering pile of hot buttered toast up the stairs to her room.

"You might bang on Danny's door and ask if he wants breakfast," Uncle Jack called after them. "On second thought, don't worry, he can make his own; he hasn't set fire to the kitchen for a few months now. If anyone needs me I'll be in the workroom. I've got a big order for Fido's Fang Polish." This was Uncle Jack's own brand of dog toothpaste. It was very popular with dogs, because it was liver flavored, though he carefully didn't specify liver of what, in case it upset people.

Ruby giggled as they shut the bedroom door and curled up on Lottie's bed with the toast. "Your uncle is so funny. Has your cousin really set the kitchen on fire?"

Lottie let Sofie answer — she'd lived with the family a lot longer than Lottie had. Danny hadn't had any major accidents since Lottie had lived there.

Sofie nodded, the toast crusts sticking out of the corners of her mouth. "Mmmpf. Twice. And when he was four, he flooded it as well. He was trying to make his mother a cup of tea in bed. He put the tea bags in the kettle, and then he left the tap running when he took the tea upstairs."

Lottie smiled sadly. Danny's mum had died when he was seven. Lottie missed her own mum, who was living in Paris at the moment, but at least she got to see her every so often, and they could talk on the phone and send e-mails. She was there in the background. Lottie couldn't imagine not having a mum at all, like Danny. At least Danny had his dad. Lottie couldn't even remember hers. He'd disappeared when she was two and had never been heard from again. She couldn't help envying that Danny had his father — well, sometimes. Uncle Jack was great, but he was so scatterbrained! He wasn't much help if you had an emergency geography project and needed a papier-mâché volcano right away.

Lottie had a feeling that Danny's mum was the kind of person who'd always made sure geography projects got done two weeks in advance. Which partly explained why Danny and Uncle Jack were now both unbelievably disorganized.

Funnily enough, Uncle Jack was very organized when it came to the shop. He never forgot to feed the animals or clean out their cages. Although of course it helped that they would complain very loudly if he did.

Lottie jumped as her bedroom door opened. Danny lurched around the door, dressed in sweatpants and an enormous sweater.

"You've got toast," he told Lottie accusingly. "I could smell it. Gimme some. Pleeease," he added, as Lottie pulled the toast closer to her. "I'm starved. Hi, Ruby." He blinked. "What time is it?"

"About nine," Lottie said. "OK, you can have one piece. And you and Sep have to share!" she added, seeing Danny's black rat appear from his sweater pocket, his whiskers quivering in anticipation of toast.

"Is there peanut butter?" Septimus inquired, leaning over to admire the toast.

"No," Lottie told him firmly. Septimus was incredibly lazy, and very persuasive, much like Danny. She knew he was quite capable of sweet-talking her into going downstairs to get it for him, probably accompanied by another five or so pieces of toast.

"What were you doing up this early?" Danny asked, dropping crumbs all over Lottie's bedspread.

"Early!" Giles the hamster tutted. "Best part of the day is before dawn." He nibbled his toast crust delicately for such a chubby creature, filling his enormous cheek pouches.

Septimus eyed him with dislike. "Hamsters, dear chap, are nocturnal. You sleep all day, when we are hard at work."

Lottie half-choked. Septimus went to school with Danny in his blazer pocket, but neither of them did any work at all.

"Lottie fought Pandora," Sofie told him proudly as she slyly sneaked another slice of toast.

"What?" Danny yelled, almost dropping his second piece, which he was hoping Lottie hadn't noticed. "Are you crazy? You went and did it on your own?"

"You knew I was going to!" Lottie protested. "You were there when I was talking to Ariadne about it."

Ariadne was Uncle Jack's girlfriend, who was a witch. She was helping Lottie find and develop her own magic. Lottie had ended up at Ariadne's apartment the previous night. After she'd found a photograph of Pandora with her father, she'd needed answers. Uncle

Jack wouldn't tell her what had happened to his brother all that time ago, but Lottie had been sure Ariadne would see that she had to know. She couldn't bear being kept in the dark any longer. Did Pandora have something to do with her dad's disappearance? It had been really weird for Lottie, finding out about her magical family, especially without her dad there. She'd inherited the magic from him, but she didn't have him around to teach her. She'd had no idea at all what had happened to him, until recently when odd things had started to happen. Ariadne knew and understood all of this, so Lottie trusted her to tell the truth.

"I wasn't going to let you go off, not without someone there for backup," Danny muttered. "I can't believe you just went off and faced her, while I was asleep!"

Lottie wasn't sure if he was mad because she'd done something dangerous, or because he'd missed an adventure, or both.

"She had me!" Sofie said in an indignant growl.

"Hamsters are always proud to be of service," Giles put in.

"And you had me too," Ruby added. "Well, I suppose I wasn't much use." She smiled at Lottie, then she shook her head. "I still can't believe Pandora put me under a spell. It's just horrible."

"*You* were horrible," Sofie told her sternly. "You were very unkind to Lottie."

Ruby looked hurt. "I'm sorry," she muttered.

"Sofie! It wasn't Ruby's fault!" Lottie put an arm around Ruby's shoulders. "I should be saying sorry to you. None of this would have happened if you hadn't been my friend. Pandora was using you to get to me, that's the kind of person she is."

"Stop arguing," Danny demanded. "What happened? I mean, you must have won. Unless you're bewitched now — are you?" He stared suspiciously at Lottie, glaring into her eyes, until she grabbed the last bit of toast and shoved it into his mouth.

"Of course we're not." Lottie looked down at her hands. "I don't honestly know what happened. How it ended, I mean, how we survived," she admitted. "It was really weird. . . . I . . . I think I saw my dad." She looked up at Danny almost shyly, not sure what he was going to think of her. She wasn't prepared for the expression of pure hurt that flashed across his face, but the moment she saw it she would have given anything to take back what she'd just said.

Danny's voice was slightly flat, but that was the only sign that she'd upset him. "I don't get it. A ghost, you mean?"

"No!" Lottie wasn't sure how she knew that her dad was alive after all, but she did. She didn't look at Danny. There wasn't an easy way to tell him. Having lost her dad, like he'd lost his mum, had always bonded them together, even though they never spoke about it. "No. I think he was real. I'm sure he was." She sighed. "But he was a unicorn." She waited for Danny to laugh. Even Ruby had thought she sounded a little crazy when she'd told her.

Danny leaned back against the wall. "OK. Tell me the whole thing."

Lottie settled her shoulders against the wall next to him and closed her eyes, remembering. "It was awful. Pandora got inside me somehow, and said she could squeeze my heart so it would stop beating —"

"She couldn't do that!" Danny scoffed. Then he looked doubtfully at Sofie. "Could she?"

Sofie shrugged. "I do not know. Perhaps. But she was not trying to. She was just scaring Lottie. And it worked."

"She was scary! I can't help it!" Lottie complained. "She terrifies me. Anyway, Sofie told me she was just pretending, and I snapped out of it, and that made Pandora so angry that she left herself open, and we slipped into her mind."

"Wow!" Ruby gasped. "You didn't tell me that! How did you do it? What was it like?"

Sitting on either side of her on the bed, the other two felt Lottie shake slightly. It frightened her even to remember. "Awful. She was so cold, like there wasn't much person left inside her anymore. She was frozen."

"We did not stay for long." Sofie laughed, a grim, grunting little chuckle.

"She threw us out, and that was — it was — there was nothing. Only black. I didn't know who I was, even." Lottie smiled gratefully at Giles, who was leaning against her pillow with his paws folded happily across his stomach. "Giles saved us."

"My paw is still not better," Sofie mourned. "I do not think you needed to bite me quite so hard."

"Sofie, dear old thing, you were both unconscious," Giles explained. "I had no choice. I am not by nature a creature of violence" — everyone spluttered slightly, as Giles was a particularly warlike hamster — "but it was necessary in this instance. You woke up, and you woke Lottie up."

"Then what happened?" Ruby asked anxiously.

Lottie frowned and bit her lip. "Then I did something stupid. I let her make me angry. She told me she had sent my dad to die. But as soon as I got angry, I was trapped. There was a fire. I mean, I know it was all in my head, but it seemed so real!"

Danny shook his head. "Elementary mistake," he said, in a disapproving, older-brotherly voice.

Lottie glared at him. "I'd like to see you taking it and not getting angry, Mr. I'm-going-to-glamour-myself-until-I-fall-off-a-skateboard!"

Danny shrugged but didn't argue. When he'd started middle school, he'd tried to use his own magic to make himself popular, but it hadn't worked very well. "Go on, then. When did the unicorn come in?"

"About then," Lottie said slowly, remembering. "I called for help. Like I did that time before, when Pandora was in my mind when I was asleep. The unicorn came that time, too, and chased her away."

Danny nodded. "Yeah, Dad mentioned that. He thought you just imagined it. You didn't say it was your dad then, though, did you?"

Lottie blinked. "No . . . I didn't realize. Come on, Danny, it was a unicorn! And everyone's always told me my dad was dead! What was I supposed to think?"

"So how do you know it was him this time? Did he say so?" Danny's face was painfully eager.

"No. He just said he'd always come if I called him, I only had to ask. But Pandora recognized him; she

11

yelled, 'You!' She screamed it out, like it was being . . . torn out of her heart. . . ." Lottie took a deep breath. "It was then that I realized who he was. Pandora sort of stepped back, and she was staring at us both. I don't think she could have hurt us; it was like she was in shock. Then I don't know what happened, but the unicorn was gone, and so was Pandora."

"But how? How could you tell it was him?" Danny demanded again, and Lottie looked at him helplessly.

"I'm sorry," she whispered. "I just could."

"I don't understand," Ruby murmured. "I mean, I don't understand any of it really, but what I don't get is why your dad turning up shocked Pandora so much. She'd tried to kill him, I guess. Was that it? She thought he was dead, and he wasn't?"

Lottie laughed, but it wasn't a happy laugh. She sounded bitter. "Sorry, Ruby, I forgot you didn't hear about that. I found it all out while you were under that spell. Pandora was my dad's old girlfriend."

"What?" Ruby squeaked. "You're kidding!"

"Nope. Ariadne told me. They went out for years. Before he met my mum. But he broke it off with her, because she was trying to control him. She tried to get between him and Uncle Jack — she was jealous, I think. Uncle Jack and my dad were really close, and she didn't want anyone to have a piece of my dad but her."

"I can believe that," Ruby muttered. "She's crazy, isn't she, totally off the charts?"

"Beyond crazy," Lottie agreed. "I thought she really hated me — I still think she does, actually. And she sent my dad off to get killed all those years ago; she laughed about it! She was gloating. But she said I looked like my dad, and maybe when he was there, too, she remembered how close they used to be." She shrugged tiredly. "I don't really understand. But I think — I think Pandora wanted to use me."

"What for?" Ruby asked plaintively. Lottie was working it all out as she went, now that she had the time to think, and it wasn't the easiest thing to follow.

"She wanted to control me. I mean, think about it. If she could get at your dad, Danny, he's the very first person who took my dad away from her. Uncle Jack was closer to my dad than she was, that's what broke them up. She's been desperate to get back at the whole Grace family ever since." Lottie stared at Danny and Ruby, her face serious. "If she could control me, and use me to hurt all of you somehow — use Tom's own daughter — it's the ultimate revenge, isn't it?"

Danny gazed back at her. "We were lucky your dad turned up when he did," he said quietly. "Even if he was wearing hooves."

13

Ruby coughed apologetically. "I'm really sorry to keep asking stupid questions, and it's probably obvious, but — *why* is he a unicorn?"

Lottie looked hopefully at Danny, but he shook his head. "Haven't a clue."

Sofie sighed. "I keep telling you all! He is *not* a unicorn! He's a dream creature. A vision. He was not really there!"

Lottie's heart suddenly pulsed with fear. "You mean, he isn't real?" she asked painfully, her eyes fixed on Sofie. "I just imagined it? But I was so sure."

Sofie shook her head so hard her ears flapped. "He is real somewhere, Lottie *chérie*, do not be afraid. And the unicorn is part of him somehow. I do not know how he is doing it. I suppose he had to pick a shape to come to you with, and that is what he chose. I wonder . . ."

"What?" the others demanded, after she trailed off in this tantalizing fashion.

"It was just a thought," Sofie mused. "I wondered if perhaps he has lost his own shape somehow — in his head, at least."

Lottie looked at her worriedly. She supposed that she ought to be grateful that her father was alive at all, considering that an hour or so ago she had been sure he was dead. But someone who had lost their shape sounded scary. Sofie's just thinking aloud, she told herself firmly. She can't be right all the time. Can she?

"Lottie! Lottie, you aren't listening!" Giles's breathy, squeaky little voice broke through to her at last, and she blinked. "No one is thinking about the important question," he told her sternly.

Lottie frowned. To her, what shape her father was seemed pretty important, but she looked inquiringly at Giles.

The plump hamster leaned in toward them all and hissed, "Where is Pandora now?" Then he sat back, paws folded, and gazed at them triumphantly.

Lottie shook her head. "I don't know," she murmured. "I sort of hoped she'd run away. But I'm not sure if she's the sort of person who does that."

"Exactly." Giles nodded, his beady little black eyes sparkling. "We need to be in a state of high alert, in case she comes back." He actually rubbed his paws together. Clearly the thought of a possible attack was just what he wanted.

Lottie wished she could be as bloodthirsty, or if not, at least as brave. The idea that Pandora could be back at any time didn't make her feel warlike. It made her want to hide under her comforter and shut out enchantresses, and fathers who had disappeared and then reappeared as mystical animals, and just everything, to be honest. Tears burned at the back of her eyes. Everything was so difficult.

Sofie nuzzled at her arm, nudging Lottie with her velvety black nose. "Do not worry, Lottie. I will not let her harm you, I promise."

The thought of a small but very determined dachshund standing up for her against Pandora made Lottie smile, even if it was rather limply. "I'll be all right," she said firmly, stroking Sofie's head. "It's only that sometimes I wish all I had to worry about was homework."

Lottie sighed, but Sofie stared back at her disapprovingly. She refused to allow Lottie self-pity. Sofie regarded wallowing as a waste of good chocolate-eating time. She shook her head at Lottie. "Well, *ma petite*, that would be very boring, do you not think?"

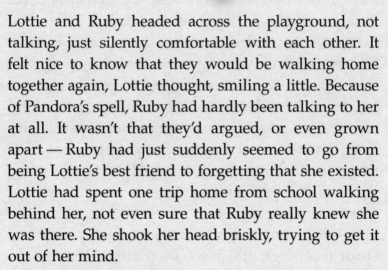

Lottie and Ruby headed across the playground, not talking, just silently comfortable with each other. It felt nice to know that they would be walking home together again, Lottie thought, smiling a little. Because of Pandora's spell, Ruby had hardly been talking to her at all. It wasn't that they'd argued, or even grown apart — Ruby had just suddenly seemed to go from being Lottie's best friend to forgetting that she existed. Lottie had spent one trip home from school walking behind her, not even sure that Ruby really knew she was there. She shook her head briskly, trying to get it out of her mind.

Ruby nudged her with her bag. "What are you thinking about?" she asked. "You look worried."

Lottie smiled at her. "Just remembering last week."

Ruby's face fell dramatically. "Lotti-eeee...," she wailed. "I've said I'm sorry! I didn't mean to, it was all the spell, honestly it was."

Lottie hugged her. "I know that, silly! I was just being glad that we were friends again."

Ruby didn't say anything for a moment. She just stared at the ground. "I didn't miss you," she said slowly. "I'm not sure I actually thought much about anyone. I didn't even realize we weren't friends anymore. Everything went blank." She glanced up at Lottie for a second to see if this had shocked her.

Lottie only nodded. "Mmmm. I suppose if Pandora had wiped half your mind away, everything that was left was just concentrating on getting through the day. Not much space left for thinking about stuff." She resisted making a jokey comment about that being pretty normal anyway; Ruby didn't seem to be in the mood. Lottie found it helped, being silly about Pandora. It was a bit too scary to think about her otherwise.

"I think you're right. I can't remember anything about that week. It's like I sleepwalked through it." Ruby shivered. "Do you think I'd have stayed like that forever, if you hadn't broken the spell?"

Lottie walked on silently for a few steps. "I honestly don't know," she admitted. "But I think maybe. Unless she had to keep thinking about the spell to make it work. What did you do with the drawing?"

"I burned it." Ruby tucked her hands under her arms, as though to stop them from shivering. Ruby had found the drawing that Pandora had used to create her spell, folded up very small in her own coat pocket that morning after Lottie fought Pandora. It was one of Ruby's mother's drawings, and it had been amazingly lifelike. Ruby stared sideways out of the page, half-smiling. Pandora had stolen it from Ruby's house, and when they found it, it had faded strangely, as though Pandora had sucked the life out of it. "Even though I knew you'd broken the spell, I couldn't bear to look at it anymore. Mum liked it more than I did anyway; she made my nose look huge." Ruby smiled a little. "She still can't work out where her sketchbook's gone. I guess Pandora just threw it away. And that's the other scary thing, Lottie. Pandora must have been inside my house to steal the sketchbook. What else did she see? That's what worries me. Did she steal something else — or — or even leave something in the house, watching us?"

Lottie shook her head. "I don't think she would have done that — she was too focused on getting you to do what she wanted, she didn't need to do anything else. But if you're worried, let Sam and Joe out of their cage one day, when your mum's shut away painting. If

Pandora left some sort of spying spell, I'll bet those two could sniff it out, no problem. It was them that worked out what was wrong with you, you know. They really watch out for you."

Ruby laughed, but she was pink with pleasure. Sam and Joe were her gorgeous blue lizards. They claimed they were a smaller species of dragon, but Lottie wasn't sure if that was just what they wanted to believe.

"They are fab, aren't they . . . ?" Ruby murmured happily. "Actually, that reminds me, they've been moaning like anything that their tank isn't warm enough now that the weather's getting colder. I promised I'd look in the pet shop down by the bridge and see if they had anything to help. I've got a horrible feeling it might mean a new tank, which would be Christmas and birthday presents for the next seventeen years. Mum still hasn't gotten over the shock of how much Sam and Joe cost in the first place."

Ruby's lizards had accidentally ended up in a huge pet shop in a big town not far from Netherbridge, where none of the staff had any idea what they were, or quite where they'd come from. Ruby's mum had agreed to buy her a hamster, but they'd walked out half an hour later with two turquoise blue dragons instead. Sam and Joe had liked the look of Ruby, and they had enough magical power to have been able to suggest very firmly that she and her mum should take them home.

Now that Lottie had told Ruby all about magic, Sam and Joe talked to her too. She adored them, even if they were nearly as bossy as Sofie.

Ruby looked at Lottie worriedly. "You don't mind, do you? I don't think your uncle's shop has stuff for lizard tanks."

"Don't be silly, of course I don't mind. Uncle Jack mostly does just the animals, and special foods and things. Can I come with you?" Lottie asked. She'd never been in the other shop. It was a normal pet shop, selling mostly pet food and bedding, that kind of thing. They had a few animals, but nothing very exciting, not that she'd heard about anyway. It would have felt a bit like betraying Uncle Jack to go and look around a different pet shop. But if Ruby wanted something that her uncle's shop didn't sell . . .

"It's nothing like your uncle's shop," Ruby warned her.

Lottie grinned. "I bet it's quieter."

"Mmm." Ruby nodded. "But now that I've seen all the pets at your place, the other one just seems really sad. I feel like all pet shops ought to have pink mice dancing the conga along the shelves."

*   *   *

The pet shop was in a row of little shops: a rather dingy cafe advertising all-you-can-eat breakfast served all day, the sort of hardware shop that sells absolutely everything, all tucked away on hundreds and hundreds of tiny shelves, and a shop that sold knitting wool, with a window full of ugly sweaters.

The pet shop's window was so covered with posters for cat foods that would give your cat fresh breath and a glossy coat, new improved dog-training whistles, cuttlefish bones, and LOST, *small white spaniel, answers to the name of Mags*, that Lottie couldn't really see much inside. The door squeaked shrilly as it swung open, and a dank smell of grubby cages rushed out at them, making Lottie grimace.

"Told you," Ruby muttered, and the door clanged shut behind them.

The shop was rather dark and muddled, but not in the nice way that Uncle Jack's shop was. There the walls were covered in cages and piles of things, but everything was clean and fresh smelling. Lottie thought Uncle Jack must have stretched the space by magic somehow, when he couldn't bear not to have some new sort of animal, because no one would have built a shop with quite so many odd corners and crannies and little strange spaces. The muddle in this shop was dusty and musty and old. The cages didn't look dirty — they were almost all empty anyway — but the underlying smell made Lottie want to sneeze.

No one was sitting behind the counter, so the girls wandered around, poking into piles to see if there was anything to do with warming up lizards in them.

"What are we actually looking for?" Lottie asked, holding a pink fluffy cat coat in dismay. No self-respecting cat would be seen dead in it. "Sort of lizard hot-water bottles?"

"I don't know," Ruby said thoughtfully. "I thought a new heat lamp for their tank — it's like artificial sunlight, you know? But Sam said what he'd really like were hot stones that he could lie on. I don't know if you can even buy those. I've a feeling that the sort of lizard they are might be used to living quite close to volcanoes."

Sam and Joe hadn't told Ruby they were actually dragons yet. Lottie thought they didn't want to upset her. Besides, with all their research into flame production, she might be a bit worried about them living in her bedroom. But now that Ruby knew everything about her uncle's pet shop, and Lottie's own magic, Lottie thought there wasn't much that could shock her. After all, she'd taken the amazing news about Lottie's dad pretty well — and that had taken some believing.

Lottie sighed. She wished she knew what to think about her father. Or what was going to happen now. It had thrown her completely, because she had known he was dead. Her mum had *always* said so. Would Lottie ever see him again? She had a feeling that she would, but when? She really wanted to know, for certain.

"What do you two want?" snapped a grumpy voice, and Lottie jumped and knocked over a stack of chew toys and a plastic Scottie wearing a plaid dog coat. She scooped them up guiltily, while a little old lady with a sour, pinched face glared at them both.

Ruby started to explain what they were looking for, while the old lady alternated between grumbling about how much she hated reptiles and glaring at Lottie.

"We've got nothing like that. Lot of nonsense," she muttered, when Ruby finished her halting description.

Ruby sighed and was just turning to leave, when something in the tottering pile behind the old woman's head caught her eye. "Oh, but look! Reptile sunlamp! You do have one, up there!" she pointed out.

The old woman looked so mad that Lottie wondered if she just hated selling things. Lottie couldn't see how the shop stayed open, if she was this nasty to everyone who came in. Or maybe she just didn't like children.

With much complaining, the old woman fetched a step stool and started to reach for the lamp. Lottie, having already knocked over one pile, decided the best thing to do was stay out of the way. She retreated back away from the counter to look at a shelf full of mouse bedding, and came face-to-face with a rabbit.

Or rather, face-to-bottom. The rabbit's cage (which looked horribly small for him) was tucked away on a big shelf between the mouse bedding and stones for the bottom of fish tanks. He was facing into one corner, looking at the wall. Lottie immediately got the sense that he wasn't happy. She wasn't sure any creature could be, all squashed up in this gloomy, miserable shop. The only other animals she'd seen were a tank of depressed-looking goldfish, with BUY ONE GET ONE FREE plastered across the front of them. Lottie thought fish were probably dim enough not to mind. But the rabbit was suffering, she could tell.

"Hey," she whispered, and the rabbit twitched a little. But he stayed staring at the wall. "Are you all right?" Lottie wasn't sure if she was expecting the rabbit to answer. Surely they wouldn't have magical creatures in this grim place? Unless it was some awful mix-up, like with Sam and Joe. Lottie felt sorry even for an ordinary pet shut up here. The rabbit peered over his shoulder hopelessly, his eyes dull. He blinked at the sight of Lottie, and his ears wiggled slightly. A faint gleam shone in his eyes, and he put his head to one side thoughtfully. Then he shuffled around so that he was looking at her properly.

"Do you like it here?" Lottie asked, waving a hand at the dusty piles of stuff around his cage.

The rabbit gave her an expressive look. *"What do you think?"* he seemed to be saying.

Lottie nodded. "It's pretty awful, isn't it . . . ?" she murmured.

"Don't bother the animals!" the old woman shouted across the shop. "I won't have the likes of you upsetting them. You ought to be ashamed of yourself!"

"Me!" Lottie shot back, spinning around. Living with her snappy, opinionated familiar Sofie, who was one very determined French dachshund, had given her much more confidence to argue with people. Even before she and Sofie had shared their magic and their thoughts, people being mean to animals had been the one thing that could make Lottie see red. She stalked back over to the counter. "I'm not upsetting him! He's miserable, can't you tell? He was just staring at the wall!" She could feel Sofie, back at home, waking up from a nap all excited. Sofie's soft black furriness wrapped around her, telling her to keep going. "He shouldn't be in a tiny little cage like that anyway."

"You mind your own business!" the old woman snapped.

"Cruelty to animals is everyone's business," Lottie told her. She had no idea where she was going with this. She didn't have enough money to buy the rabbit, and she was sure that the rabbit wasn't actually being treated badly enough that she could report the shop to the SPCA or anywhere like that. He was just miserable.

"Cruelty! Right. Both of you, out of my shop, this minute. Cheeky little devils, I'll have the police on you!" And the old woman surged around the counter in a rush and hurried them out, squawking and gobbling like an angry, scrawny-necked chicken.

As she bustled them out the door, Lottie looked back and saw the rabbit sadly turning around to face the wall again. That one glance back decided it.

She was going to get him out of there.

Unfortunately she had absolutely no idea how.

"Wow," Ruby murmured as the door squeaked shut again in a determined manner. "She wasn't a witch or anything, was she?"

"No, she was just mean," Lottie said, staring back into the pet shop window and resisting the urge to make faces. The old lady was still staring at them, and she was holding her telephone with her finger poised meaningfully over the buttons. "I suppose we shouldn't have let her shove us out, but I couldn't see how to stop her. I mean, it is her shop, and she hadn't actually done anything wrong."

"You were right, though," Ruby told her. "The rabbit did look totally depressed."

"Oh good, I'm glad you thought so, too, and I wasn't just overreacting." Lottie looked back through the window. "Come on. Let's go back to our shop. I want to ask Uncle Jack if there's anything we can do."

They set off, walking slowly and looking back at the dirty windows of the shop every so often. "I hate to leave him there," Lottie muttered. "He looked so hopeless. The way he just turned around to the wall again. I bet he never gets taken out of that cage for a cuddle."

"He wasn't a talking rabbit, was he?" Ruby asked.

Lottie wrinkled her nose, looking quite like a rabbit herself for a moment. "I don't think so. . . . But even if he was, with no one around to talk to him, and stuck in that awful place, he might have forgotten how to. Or just never learned, like Tabitha the cat hadn't. There was something about him. He had such lovely eyes. Really big and soft looking, almost like he could talk with those."

"We can't leave him there," Ruby said firmly. "I guess we could buy him."

"Have you got any money?" Lottie asked hopefully.

Ruby shook her head. "Sam and Joe are really expensive to feed. I have to buy them locusts, and, um, mice and stuff...." She knew how much Lottie loved mice, so she didn't like to mention Sam and Joe's eating habits.

"Ugh." Lottie shuddered. "I'm really glad Uncle Jack only has small lizards. Imagine our mice watching the lizards having lunch, that would be awful." She sighed. "I haven't any money either. And I'm not sure she'd sell the rabbit to us, anyway, just out of spite. I suppose we could send Danny."

"Or I could ask my dad, if we explained," Ruby suggested. "He really likes animals; he'd understand. It's just that he's so busy with work, I hardly get to see him."

"Mmm." Lottie thought about Ruby's dad. At least when Ruby saw him, he was real. Lottie wondered what her own dad was doing right now. It was so odd to think that she had seen him over the weekend, just like any other person whose dad didn't live with them all the time.

Lottie still didn't know people very well at the school in Netherbridge, but at her old school, at least a third of the class didn't live with both their mum and dad. Lots of people had half brothers and sisters. It had made it easier for Lottie. No one had been very surprised that her dad wasn't around. Quite a few of her friends weren't there for sleepovers and stuff on the weekends because they'd gone to see their dads.

But then, their dads were just living in an apartment somewhere a little way away, they weren't lost in the rain forests of the Himalayas chasing unicorns. And when Lottie had seen her dad, he'd actually *been* a unicorn. Somehow. And he hadn't really been there, he was just a vision, or so Sofie said.

"It's not just the rabbit making you miserable, is it? Are you worrying about your dad again?" Ruby asked her gently, touching her arm.

Lottie blinked at her, coming slowly out of the memory, her eyes hot and scratchy with tears. She nodded. It wasn't fair to resent Ruby because she saw her dad every day, even if it wasn't for very long. One tear dripped down Lottie's nose as she thought again how much luckier she was than Danny. His face flashed into her mind, that look of loss when she'd told him what she'd seen. Her dad *was* alive, after all. His mum wasn't going to stage a magical reappearance.

But still, she almost envied Danny too. At least he was certain what was going on with his family. He'd actually seen his mum buried. He went to visit her grave sometimes, with flowers. And his dad was there with him every day, even if he was a bit ditzy. He was *there*. Not off in another country for work. One parent missing is understandable, Lottie thought. But losing both of them, Lottie, that's just careless.

"I just wish I knew what's going to happen," Lottie whispered. "If he's coming back or not. Maybe he can't. Will I ever see him for real? I know he's alive, but I still don't ever get to hug him, or have him come to the school for parents' night, or anything." She stared at Ruby, hating to say it, but desperate to tell someone. "I'm not sure I wouldn't rather he was still dead," she said in a rush. "I can't stand this not knowing. It doesn't make me feel better that he's alive. It just makes me feel sick."

3

When Lottie and Ruby got back to Grace's Pet Shop, Lottie scrubbing her eyes determinedly with a grungy-looking tissue she'd found at the bottom of her coat pocket, they couldn't help smiling at its difference from the shop by the bridge. As they pushed open the door, one of the pink mice was standing on the counter, demonstrating to Uncle Jack and Ariadne that he really could balance an acorn on his nose. He froze as the doorbell jingled, and the acorn fell off, very slowly, and plinked across the counter.

"Oh, it's you!" Fred the mouse scolded. "I nearly went white! Could you try *not* to do that sort of thing?"

"Sorry," Lottie told him, grinning. Fred always cheered her up.

"You're late, girls," Uncle Jack commented.

"Lottie came to help me look for a new sunlamp for Sam and Joe," Ruby explained. "We — er — we went to that other pet shop down by the bridge?" She looked worriedly at Uncle Jack, hoping he wouldn't be annoyed.

Uncle Jack frowned slightly. "What was it like?" he asked. "I haven't been past it recently, but it's always looked a bit dingy to me."

"It was horrible," Lottie told him.

"They had a lamp, but it wasn't as good as the one Sam and Joe have now," Ruby added.

"Did they have any animals?" Uncle Jack looked anxious. "I hope not; it looks so depressing in there."

Lottie nodded. "Not many. There was a fish tank, and the fish looked OK, but there was a rabbit, too, Uncle Jack, and I'm really worried about him."

"A rabbit?" Uncle Jack looked thoughtful. "A white one?"

"No, a sort of soft gray, and really sweet. He had enormous twitchy ears. He hated it in there, you could tell." Lottie's voice shook. The rabbit had made her feel so sad, and so angry at the same time. No one should be allowed to keep an animal in a tiny cage like that.

There was a brisk flurry of clicking sounds, as Sofie galloped down the stairs and skidded into the shop. "Lottie! You're back! If only I'd been with you, I could have bitten that woman for you," she told Lottie sadly. "Why were you so angry with her? I was half-asleep, I couldn't tell."

"She was being cruel to a rabbit," Lottie explained, picking Sofie up and hugging her.

"Lottie told her off," Ruby added. "You'd have been proud of her."

Sofie sniffed. "Rabbits are useless. All they can do is jump out of hats. What is the point of that, hmm?"

Ariadne laughed. "I think humans make them do that, Sofie, because they think it's funny. I don't think rabbits actually *like* hats very much."

"Well then, they should not do it," Sofie said dismissively. "Why are we bothering with this rabbit, Lottie? I am not interested in boring rabbits. They have no conversation."

"I'm not sure this is actually a rabbit that can talk at all," Lottie admitted. "But it's trapped in a little cage in a grubby pet shop, Sofie. It was really beautiful, with gorgeous big eyes, like yours, only really sparkly. It was so sad, shut away like that. We have to bother with it."

Sofie blinked at this description, and seemed about to say something. Then she shrugged, which was quite a major operation for such a small dog. Her shrug started with her ears and went all the way to her tail. "Oh well, if you say so," she agreed, in a most uninterested voice.

Lottie was rather shocked. She knew that Sofie was lazy and chocolate-obsessed, but she hadn't thought that she wouldn't care about another animal being badly treated. In fact, only a couple of months before, Sofie had helped her rescue Tabitha, the little brown tabby cat who was now Ariadne's familiar. At the time, they had both thought that Tabitha was just a grubby stray. Who knew what this rabbit could be?

Tabitha sensed that Lottie was thinking about her. Ariadne was sitting on the edge of the shopwindow, and Tabitha had been dozing in the velvet bag at her side. She woke up with an enormous yawn and stepped delicately out of the bag, blinking.

Fred immediately whisked back up the shelves to the safety of his cage, spitting mouse insults. "You didn't tell me she was here!" he squeaked angrily at Ariadne. "I could have been mortally wounded. Two shocks in one day; my coat will never be the same again."

Tabitha jumped gracefully onto the counter and politely touched noses with Sofie. They tolerated each other, but they would never be friends. She purred at Lottie and Ruby, which made Sofie's whiskers bristle.

"Isn't Shadow with you?" Lottie asked, and Ariadne and Tabitha exchanged a worried glance.

"He was too tired," Ariadne explained. "We left him back at the apartment, sleeping."

"Again," Tabitha mewed. "It's all he does these days," she added in a mutter.

Ariadne sighed and stroked her gently. "I know it's boring for you. But he's such an old cat. He needs to rest."

Tabitha jumped back onto Ariadne's lap and rubbed her head lovingly against her mistress's cheek. "I know. I'm only grumpy because I'm worried about him," she murmured. Then she turned around to eye Sofie and Lottie. "You ought to help this rabbit," she told them. "If you hadn't helped me, I would never have found Ariadne. And she would probably have ended up with that frightful Selina as her new familiar."

There was a grumpy hiss from the next room, where the black cats, Selina and Sarafan, had their pen.

"Another thing to do," Uncle Jack muttered, tying a knot in his handkerchief. "I must find those two an owner; they shouldn't be shut up in that pen all the time, at their age."

"But Uncle Jack," Lottie complained, "their pen is huge! I know they're actually locked in it, and most of the animals aren't, but it's still like a great big cat palace! You should have seen the tiny little cage this rabbit was in."

Uncle Jack looked apologetic. "I know, Lottie. But rabbits are used to being shut up, and cats aren't. They're free-range pets. I only keep Selina and Sarafan penned up because *I can't trust them!*" He said the last bit in a very meaningful voice, and a sneering little purr answered him from across the shop.

Not only were the two cats extremely greedy and prone to chasing and, if possible, eating anything that moved, they were also master criminals. They were now up to six padlocks on their pen, and the latest one had a combination number. Every time anyone walked past the pen, the cats would ask them seemingly idle questions about birthdays and house numbers, and if the person was foolish enough to answer, they would go into a huddle and start frantically working out possible combinations. Whenever the shop was quiet, one could hear a gentle *click-click-click* of tumblers turning, as the cats delicately manipulated the lock. Lottie happened to know that Uncle Jack had actually set the combination as 1234, because he hated that sort of thing and always forgot numbers. Luckily, Selina and Sarafan were far too devious to believe that anyone would use a code that simple, so they would probably never find it out.

"This rabbit didn't like being shut up, Uncle Jack," Lottie assured him. "He was really miserable. Can't we rescue him somehow?"

"He looked ever so sad," Ruby agreed.

Ariadne and Uncle Jack looked at each other. "Well, I suppose you could try a calling spell," Ariadne suggested.

"Good idea." Uncle Jack nodded happily. "And good practice too."

"How does it work?" Lottie asked eagerly. "I could go and try it now."

"Homework," Horace the parrot grunted warningly from his perch in the window. He had taken it upon himself to educate Lottie, since he'd tested her on her spelling words and discovered she still mixed up *threw* and *through*. He thought she wasn't being taught very well, and kept reciting Latin grammar at her when she wasn't expecting it. He swore it would come in handy one day.

"I promise I'll do my history first," Lottie assured him. "We've got to look up something about Egyptians on the computer, that's all. I can be thinking about the spell while I'm doing that, though, can't I?"

"Computer," Horace growled dismissively. "Lot of nonsense. Can you girls recite all the kings and queens of England? You cannot. Shameful."

"But I know the Egyptians used to pull dead people's brains out of their noses with a special hook," Lottie told him brightly. "That's much more useful."

Horace turned his back on her and ruffled his feathers irritably. Ruby giggled.

Ariadne sniffed. "Ridiculous idea. Completely pointless thing to do. Anyway. For a calling spell you need to think very carefully about the creature you're calling," she explained. "Especially think about its magical self. Try and call to that. You might find you need a picture to look at, and sometimes fresh herbs can put you in the right mood. You remember the ones we talked about?"

Lottie frowned. "But I'm not sure this rabbit *is* magical. How can I think about its magical self if it doesn't have one?"

"Oh . . ." Ariadne looked blank. "I hadn't thought of that. I usually work with magical animals."

"It might work with an everyday rabbit, if you think hard enough about what made him special," Uncle Jack mused. "You mentioned his ears, and his sparkly eyes. Remember that sort of thing, and call. Sofie can help. I know she didn't see him, but having your familiar with you helps you make your spells stronger."

Lottie looked doubtfully at Sofie, who was staring vaguely out the window. She didn't seem in the slightest bit interested in making any spells stronger. Not those to do with rabbits, anyway.

"I'd better get home, Mum'll be looking out for me,"

Ruby said, picking up her schoolbag. "Meet you by the bridge before school tomorrow, Lottie, OK?"

Lottie waved good-bye to her and looked around to ask Sofie if she wanted to share a banana while they looked up stuff on the computer. But oddly, Sofie had disappeared.

She didn't turn up all evening, and Lottie worried, getting more and more upset. Sofie *knew* she wanted to try the calling spell. Where had she gone? Lottie was actually forced to do some homework in advance, and she was so grumpy she didn't even feel virtuous.

Sofie eventually sneaked through her bedroom door, looking innocent, just as Lottie was about to go brush her teeth.

"Where have you *been*?" Lottie demanded, her voice squeaking with anger.

"I was busy," Sofie retorted, stalking across the rug with her nose in the air and scrambling up onto the bed.

"But the spell!" Lottie folded her arms and glared.

"We can do it tomorrow." Sofie's voice was muffled. She was curled into a velvety black doughnut shape, her nose buried under her tail. She wasn't moving.

Lottie huffed in exasperation and went off to the bathroom.

*   *   *

Maybe it was the anger and frustration with Sofie that opened her mind, or maybe it was that Sofie had withdrawn herself a little, leaving the way to Lottie's mind open, but that night, Lottie dreamed.

More than a dream. A vision. A message.

Lottie was thundering across the ground under a starlit sky, her feet thudding. No, her hooves. Lottie had a moment of horrible panic, where her galloping stride caught and stumbled. She was a unicorn now too!

"Don't fall, little one." Someone was galloping beside her. Someone had slowed their breakneck pace to nudge her onward. Lottie strode out gratefully, matching her pace to the larger creature beside her. Her long mane floated out behind her in the whirlwind of her gallop, and her ivory hooves beat out a strong, confident rhythm. Lottie relaxed into her run, smiling inside.

"Good, isn't it?" asked her father beside her. She knew it was him, and she could hear that he was smiling too.

"I think I could do this forever," Lottie told him breathlessly.

There was a tinge of sadness in his voice as he replied. "I thought that, too, Lottie, I thought that too."

They slowed gradually, to a canter, then a walk, then they stood, staring out through the leafless winter trees, across a shining midnight lake.

Still now, Lottie shook out her golden mane — it seemed she was a golden unicorn, unlike her father's silver — and admired its silky curls. It smelled good, too, like Christmas spices. She cast a satisfied look back over her smooth coat, and flicked her waterfall of a tail. She looked like she had been polished.

"You're very beautiful," her father told her. "So tall. I've been away a long time. . . ." He was smiling again, but a little sadly.

"Is it nice to be a unicorn?" Lottie asked, wondering if she could stay. No more questions, only running under the moonlight.

"No." Her father was silent for a moment. "It's wonderful. But it isn't what we're meant to be, Lottie. Do you really want to leave everyone behind?"

Lottie blinked, long, golden lashes flicking over her deep brown eyes. "No. Not Mum, and Sofie. Ruby. Even Danny. I couldn't."

"Exactly. You should always go back."

"Are you coming back?" Lottie asked hopefully.

"I'm trying, Lottie, I promise. It's hard."

The quiet moonlight faded, replaced by a groaning engine noise and a stinging, salty wind.

Now she was on a boat — no, a ship. A large one that smelled strange, like car exhaust but worse. She guessed it was the engine. There was a strong undertone of fish too. She was leaning over the side rail, staring down at the gray water.

She could feel him standing beside her, but he didn't speak. Maybe he didn't know she was there.

Carefully, shyly, wondering if he would disappear as soon as she looked, Lottie glanced up.

Her father!

Really him this time, not the strange, silvery white unicorn she'd seen before. Lottie's heart jumped, and she reached out her hand, hesitantly stroking the sleeve of his yellow oilskin jacket.

He couldn't feel her. Lottie sighed. It had been the same when she'd visited her mother in Paris once, walking through a magical door that Sofie had found in the pet shop. It had led them out into another shop, full of glittering birds flying free under a painted ceiling. A Paris pet shop, only a few streets from her mother's apartment.

When she and Sofie had climbed the fire escape and sneaked in through her mother's kitchen window, Lottie had rushed to hug her. Seeing her mum crying because she was missing her so much, Lottie'd forgotten that she wasn't meant to be there, that her mum would be full of questions. Lottie had only thought of holding her. But her mother couldn't tell she was there. Lottie was sure she'd felt *something*, but she and Sofie had been invisible, like ghosts. It was a good thing, really; it would have been so hard to explain how she'd gotten there — impossible, probably. But she had wanted a real hug, all the same.

Now her father couldn't feel her either. It meant she wasn't really there, Lottie supposed. Still keeping her fingers on him — did she think he was going to float away? — Lottie took a little step backward and looked up. Her father was very tall. She'd vaguely remembered that about him, but she hadn't believed it from her baby memories, thinking that he was tall only because she was so small. He still was, though. He was very tan, much more so than Uncle Jack, who liked to say he was a troll, hiding away from sunshine in his shop. Lottie supposed that if he'd been in India, or somewhere close to India, anyway, then he would be tan. His hair was still black and curly, like hers, with just the odd silvery, wiry thread here and there.

His hands, folded on his arms as he leaned on the rail, had long, thin fingers, just like Lottie's. She caught her breath, staring at them. Daddy. She hadn't thought she remembered much, but she remembered those hands, making paper airplanes for her, doing

44

the actions of the silly baby songs she'd liked to sing. Lottie moved her hand from his sleeve and laid it over the long fingers, dragging up all her love and hope, and sending it through her skin to speak to him.

He blinked. But that was all. He might just have had dry eyes from the sea wind.

Lottie sighed. At least he was on a boat. That had to be good, didn't it? He was traveling. Surely that meant he was coming home? The unicorn had said he was trying. This dream had to be a message, to show he was on his way back to her.

It was so frustrating, not being able to talk to him. Lottie almost wished he was a unicorn again — at least then he'd be able to see her, wouldn't he? And they could talk?

She almost wished it, but not quite. Seeing the real him was so amazing. He looked so like all those pho- tographs. Like a taller, skinnier Uncle Jack. It was like seeing a fading memory come alive again. She couldn't let it go, even if he couldn't talk to her.

Her father turned around and leaned against the rail, now staring up into the sky. He muttered some- thing that Lottie couldn't quite hear, and she pressed in close against him, staring at his lips, willing him to say it again.

"She's after me. I can feel her coming. I don't know what she wants." He shook his head wearily. "What if she finds what I'm searching for?" He pressed his hands against his eyes, muttering angrily. "What *am* I searching for? I can't see, I can't see. Where are they all?"

Lottie put her arms around him, wishing he knew she was there. He had to be talking about Pandora, she was sure. Well, that answered her question. Pandora wasn't going to leave them alone. But she wasn't just coming back for Lottie. Now that she knew Lottie's dad was still alive, she was going after him instead.

4

Lottie woke up shaking, her hands stretching out to keep hold of her father, but he slipped away from her with sleep.

"What's the matter?" Sofie asked, wriggling grumpily as Lottie woke her, and Lottie suddenly realized that she and her father had been alone in the dream. Since Lottie and Sofie had bonded, Lottie hardly ever dreamed without Sofie there too.

"I was with my dad," she murmured to Sofie, watching her yawn and stretch in the half-light.

Sofie stopped midstretch and padded up the bed closer to her. "I do not understand. I was asleep. How could you go without me?"

The words were accusing, but Sofie's voice was somehow worse. She didn't sound as though she was trying to make Lottie feel guilty — she sounded lost, and bewildered, and desperately hurt.

"I don't know," Lottie told Sofie flatly. She knew that she should be conciliatory, comforting Sofie, reassuring her. But half her mind was still on that ship, staring out at the huge amount of sky and sea, and trying to make her father see her.

Sofie gave a pitiful little whine and went down to the end of the bed, where she tucked her nose under her paws, as though she was trying to hide.

Lottie lifted her head slowly. "Sofie, I'm sorry, I really don't know why you didn't come with me. I didn't mean it to happen that way. I just had a dream! Please don't be angry with me." She sighed wearily. She didn't feel as though she'd actually slept at all.

" 'M not angry," Sofie muttered, from under her paws.

"Well, upset, then."

"You left me behind."

"I didn't mean to!" Lottie wailed, and jumped as Danny thumped on the wall from his bedroom next door to tell her to stop making that awful noise at this hour of the morning.

"We should go back to sleep. You have school." Sofie turned her back on Lottie, and when Lottie tried to reach her mind, she was met by a soft, blank fog that screamed *sleep*, in a most unsleepy way.

When Lottie woke up again, Uncle Jack's shout dragging her out of a shallow, restless sleep, Sofie was gone. Lottie threw on her school uniform and clattered down the stairs anxiously.

Sofie was drinking coffee in the kitchen. There were coffee bubbles on her nose, but she didn't have her usual first-caffeine-hit-of-the-day expression of bliss. Her whiskers had a decided droop. When she saw Lottie watching her from the doorway, she shook her ears briskly and tried to look unconcerned.

"Are you OK?" Lottie whispered, grabbing a glass and some juice, and sitting down next to her.

"Of course. Why would I not be?" Sofie asked airily.

Lottie didn't know what to say to break through her don't-care front, but she desperately wanted to, because she was sure Sofie did care, very much. "I have to get to school," she sighed. "I'll see you later. Will you try and help me with this calling spell, for the rabbit? Please?"

Sofie stared into her coffee. "Very well," she muttered ungraciously.

Lottie walked to meet Ruby at the bridge more slowly than she should have. She was trying to figure out why Sofie was being so grumpy about helping this rabbit. Did she really just not like rabbits? But she had helped Tabitha the cat, and Sofie hated cats! It didn't make sense. And why had Sofie not been in her dream last night? All Lottie could think was that it was because they had quarreled with each other just before she went to sleep. Had it really made that much difference?

They'd disagreed with each other before. Though mostly only over who got the last chocolate. Lottie had been sure that Sofie being her familiar meant they would always be together — they were part of each other. That couldn't stop! Or at least, she hoped it couldn't. . . .

Lottie kicked moodily through the autumn leaves and stomped onto the bridge to meet Ruby.

"Hey. Good morning to you too." Ruby grinned. She was wearing a crazy red woolen hat with a huge pompom that clashed with her red curls so badly it looked really good. Lottie wished she had the guts to wear something like that.

"What's up?" Ruby asked as they walked on.

"Sofie's in a mood with me. I had another dream-visit from my dad last night, and I did it without her. She thinks I left her behind on purpose."

"And you didn't?" Ruby checked.

Lottie gave a short little laugh. "Nope. I didn't even know *I* was going. I couldn't have left her if I'd tried. She just didn't come."

"Did he tell you anything more? Was he still, um, a unicorn?" Ruby was a bit doubtful about the whole unicorn thing, but Lottie could see why. She didn't fully understand it herself.

"He was both. He started off as a unicorn, but then I saw the real him." Lottie smiled for the first time that morning. "I think he's coming home, Ruby. He was on a ship. But he didn't know I was there. And he thinks someone's chasing him. 'Her,' he said. It has to be Pandora, doesn't it?"

"I guess so." Ruby shuddered. "Great. Just what we need. But it's good news, Lottie, isn't it? That your dad's coming home? You just don't sound as happy as I thought you would."

Lottie sighed. "I wish he'd recognized me, that's all. When he was on the ship, he couldn't even see me. And I'm really worried about Sofie. And that poor rabbit." She glanced back over her shoulder. They couldn't quite see the pet shop from here, but she knew the rabbit was close by, still staring at the wall behind his cage, she was sure. "We have to get him away from there," she muttered to Ruby.

"Did you try the spell that Ariadne suggested? Didn't it work?"

"I couldn't do it; Sofie disappeared last night. I was really upset with her. I think that might be why I went on that dream-journey without her, because I was still mad. And I really need her to help with the spell. Especially if he isn't a magic rabbit; it'll be even harder then." Lottie frowned. "Ruby, do you think Uncle Jack's right, and rabbits don't mind being shut up? Ones who aren't magical, I mean? Uncle Jack didn't seem to care as much when he thought it was just any old rabbit. Sofie certainly didn't. Why should magic animals be more important?"

Ruby wrinkled her nose. "Maybe magic animals feel things more?" she suggested, shrugging. "But you're right, it doesn't seem fair. Poor old thing. Lottie . . ." Ruby hesitated, and lowered her voice. They were getting close to school, and the street was crowded with children hurrying along. "Maybe we should just steal him?"

Lottie stared at her, trying to tell if she was serious. "Do you mean it?"

"Well, I bet we could," Ruby said thoughtfully. "I don't think it would be that difficult, if we watched the shop and waited till she went out to the back. It didn't look like the sort of shop that had security cameras, did it? And the cage wasn't locked."

"But it's . . . well . . . *wrong*," Lottie said helplessly.

"It's wrong to be cruel to animals, like you said," Ruby retorted. "Anyway. If the spell doesn't work, that's what I think we should do."

Lottie followed her friend through the school gates, thinking, not for the first time, that Ruby was ever so much braver than she was. Ruby saw what she thought was right and did it, even if it meant doing something wrong along the way.

It was very courageous — but Lottie hoped whole-heartedly that the spell would work after all. Stealing would be their last resort.

As they walked into the classroom, someone shoved Lottie, and she fell against the door frame, yelping as her shoulder hit the wood. Ruby, who was in front, shot back and grabbed her and hauled her up, glaring at the person behind.

"Oh, Lottie, I'm so sorry, I slipped," Zara Martin said sweetly, as she picked up Lottie's bag for her.

Lottie stared angrily into Zara's deep, dark blue eyes, which were wide with innocence. She was a pink-cheeked, brown-haired, angelic-looking girl, always surrounded by a gang of friends who hung on her every word.

Lottie looked at Zara's eyes and saw herself reflected in them, looking small and pale. That's what she makes me, Lottie thought. That's where she wants me anyway. Then another thought flitted in: Her eyes are hard, like glass mirrors.

She smiled charmingly at Zara, and saw the reflection change, from a washed-out looking color to a true picture. Lottie had cast a strong spell on Zara a few weeks before, one that had shaken Zara's position as everyone's favorite, or at least, everyone's princess. Lottie was fairly sure no one in the class actually liked her that much. But she'd been alternately bullying and charming all of them since nursery school, and they'd grown into the habit of obedience.

Zara's pretty mouth twisted in a hard line as she realized Lottie wasn't scared of her. "Are you going to stand in the door all day?" she snapped.

Lottie walked slowly to her table, turning her back on Zara, even though that felt like a bad thing to do — like turning one's back on a snake about to strike.

"I told you that you shouldn't have let her forget what you did!" Ruby hissed as Lottie sat down. "She's as bad as ever!"

Lottie shook her head. "No, she doesn't scare me like she used to. She's definitely rattled. She knows that no one worships her quite as much as they used to, but she doesn't know why. And she hates not knowing." Lottie couldn't help sounding a little smug, but then she had been very proud of that spell.

Lottie smiled to herself. As Zara had pushed her, she'd felt a dart of worry from Sofie, responding to Lottie falling. Sofie might be upset with her, but they were still joined, and Sofie still cared about her. She thought lovingly of Sofie, and received back a message of a sleepy dog curled up on the old armchair in the kitchen. Apparently the shop was irritatingly busy, and Sofie didn't want to be disturbed. *Pay attention, Lottie,* she scolded, yawning and turning around more comfortably on the chair. *You are supposed to be working.*

Lottie's smugness was nothing compared to Sofie's.

Because Lottie was ahead with her homework, it meant that as soon as she got home from school she could start work on the spell. Lottie grinned to herself as she dumped her schoolbag in the kitchen. She supposed Mrs. Laurence had to be right occasionally. She was always lecturing the fifth graders about not leaving their work till the last minute.

Sofie was still in the armchair, and Lottie suspected that she might not have moved all day, except perhaps to consume a small snack or three at lunchtime.

"I know you aren't asleep," Lottie told her firmly. "Come on, we need to go try out that spell."

Sofie rolled onto her back and waved her paws in the air pathetically. Her shiny black nails sparkled. "I am hungry," she moaned. "Magic is most fatiguing. I will need chocolate. Lots of chocolate." A bright, roguish eye peeked at Lottie, before she closed them both again, so as to look suitably weary.

"We've run out of the last box from Mum," Lottie told her. "But I bought you a bar on the way home from school, OK?"

Sofie sat up very quickly. "Milk or dark?"

"The kind with the nutty stuff in the middle."

"Oh, very well, then." Sofie leaped lightly down from the chair and pranced off to the stairs. "I hope it is a *large* bar; this spell sounded very difficult," she called back.

When Lottie reached her room, Sofie was sitting expectantly on the bed, the very tip of her bright pink tongue sticking out. She stared hopefully at Lottie's pockets.

Lottie pulled out the bar of chocolate and unwrapped it, breaking off a large piece.

Sofie leaned toward it hungrily.

"Just this one bit," Lottie told her, "and the rest after we've done the spell. Or at least tried to. OK?"

Sofie nodded vigorously and accepted the chocolate with a rapturous expression, closing her eyes and sighing deeply. It lasted about ten seconds, then her eyes snapped open and she barked, "More!"

"No! I told you, no more until we've done the spell." Lottie frowned.

"Oh, Lottie, just one more piece," Sofie pleaded, her head to one side, fluttering her eyelashes.

"No! You can lay on all the charm you want, I won't give you any." Lottie folded her arms firmly and glared at Sofie. She could feel that Sofie was trying to persuade her with magic. Her fingers itched to open the paper wrapper again. "Sofie, stop it! That's rude!"

Sofie huffed impatiently. "I am *very* hungry," she complained. "One little piece would not have hurt. Come on, then, let us do this silly spell, if we must."

Lottie sat down beside her, putting the chocolate in the drawer of her bedside table.

"We have to think about the rabbit. Picture him, Uncle Jack said." She put her hand on Sofie's back, feeling the warmth of her fur, and closed her eyes hopefully, waiting for the images to flood into her mind. They didn't.

"I cannot picture him," Sofie complained. "I did not see him."

Lottie sighed. "Can't you just think of a rabbit? He was gray, with sweet twitchy ears."

Sofie scowled. "No. I do not like rabbits. Silly little white fluffy tails they have."

"Sofie, I need you to help me, please," Lottie begged. "I can't do this without you." She was half buttering Sofie up, but half of her really meant it. She needed Sofie's power, and her familiarity with magic, to push the spell out of her mind and into the real world.

Sofie smiled. Dogs can't smile in quite the same way as humans, they don't have the lips for it, but Sofie managed. It was a supremely satisfied little smirk. "Oh, very well," she said carelessly. "If you really cannot manage without me."

Lottie closed her eyes again, staring into the sparkling darkness behind her eyelids, and tried to remember the little gray rabbit. It was the expression in his eyes that she remembered most clearly, the way that at first there had been no life in them; then, when he saw that Lottie was actually interested in him, the look of amazement he'd given her as he turned around to see her clearly.

Lightly stroking Sofie's back, she imagined the softer fur of the rabbit, and waited for Sofie's strong magic to help her. "Rabbits!" she whispered to Sofie, still trying to concentrate.

Reluctantly, slowly, a surge of magic from Sofie joined her own. Lottie began to build a picture of a little gray rabbit, with sad brown eyes, floating in the air in front of them, like the image she had made of Zara. When he was there, and real, she would be able to call to him. But he was still too misty and wobbly, and the color wasn't quite right. She drew on more of Sofie's magic. Soft, chocolaty brown fur. Chocolate eyes.

Chocolate whiskers.

"He had white whiskers," Lottie murmured to herself. But the whiskers stayed obstinately chocolate, and the rabbit had a white-chocolate tail, and white-chocolate eyes. . . .

Lottie's eyes flew open. "Sofie! This isn't an Easter bunny! It's a real rabbit, not one made of chocolate."

"I cannot help it," Sofie muttered sulkily, her black eyes flashing with irritation. "I am hungry, and I want that chocolate, and I do not know what the rabbit looks like. I know what chocolate looks like. If you want me to help, you will have to feed me properly," she added, with her nose in the air. "If you fed me properly, I might have fur as soft as a rabbit's."

Lottie blinked at her. "Are you jealous?" she asked in amazement.

"Of course not!" Sofie snapped, but she wouldn't look at Lottie, and her voice was too loud.

"Sofie, is that why you won't try to do this correctly, because you don't want us to rescue the rabbit? You're jealous of him?"

Sofie said nothing. She looked mulishly out the window.

"That's stupid!" Lottie burst out. "You don't need to be jealous! Sofie, I love you. Helping that rabbit escape from somewhere horrible isn't going to change that!"

Sofie's ears twitched when Lottie said she loved her, but she didn't move. Instead, she sent Lottie a fleeting glimpse of herself cuddling a rabbit (which was extremely ugly) while Sofie herself stood on her hind legs, sadly scratching at Lottie's knee with one trembling paw. Lottie was ignoring her.

"Oh, that's so unfair!" Lottie burst out. She glared at Sofie, who still wouldn't look at her. "Fine. If that's how you're going to be." Lottie closed her eyes again and leaned back against the wall. She wasn't as skilled with mind-pictures as Sofie, and she needed to concentrate.

This is what it's like for the rabbit, Sofie. This is what it might be like for you, if you had an owner who didn't love you.

Sofie was lying on a cushion in the corner of a kitchen, watching with nervous eyes as a little girl sorted through a basket of doll's clothes.

"There! I knew it was the right size." She seized triumphantly on a small pink dress and a bonnet, and flung her doll to the floor. "Come here, Sofie!"

Sofie yelped and shot off her cushion, racing into the hallway, and the little girl hurtled after her, shrieking, "Sofie! Bad dog! Come back, come back here this minute!"

Sofie raced into the living room and scooted under the

sofa, pressing herself to the back. She hid there, trembling and whimpering under her breath, while the little girl stamped and cried and begged her to come out.

"Crystal! It's time for school, come and put your coat on!" another voice called from the hallway, and the little girl got up, grumbling, and Sofie heard her stomping out of the room.

She crept to the front of the sofa, listening cautiously. If they really were off to school, she would have a few hours' peace until Crystal came back. She would be able to relax and sleep without having to keep one eye open.

She heard Crystal's mother in the hall, asking, "Did you remember to feed the dog, Crystal, and let her out?"

"Yes," Crystal told her, not even listening.

She hadn't, of course, Sofie thought hungrily. Had she been fed last night? She wasn't sure. She was used to going hungry. When they did remember to feed her, they opened little cans that smelled strange, but she ate them. She preferred the smell of her owners' food, but she wasn't allowed to have it; she only got it occasionally when Crystal didn't want something and she would feed it to Sofie under the table. It was usually vegetables, but even so, it was nice to have a change from food that was always brown.

She wriggled out from under the sofa and limped back to her cushion. She had banged her paw on the door when she *was running away from the pink dress. She wondered sadly if Crystal's mother might take her for a walk today. It was sunny, and it would be so nice to be outside, even if her paw did hurt.*

Quietly, Sofie curled up on her cushion, burying her nose under her paws, and trying to dream of another home, a home where she was loved.

Lottie opened her eyes and looked at Sofie, who was staring back at her in horror.

"You want me to have another home?" Sofie whispered. "You want me to belong to someone else?"

Lottie had never seen her look so sad. She looked like the dream Sofie cowering under the sofa, her ears drooping. Lottie sighed and reached out a hand to Sofie. But Sofie drew back, trembling.

"Sofie! Of course I don't. I just wanted you to see that it isn't fair! Why shouldn't that rabbit have a home where he's loved too?"

"You do not love me anymore," Sofie said, with dismal certainty. "You want a rabbit to be your familiar instead. So he can jump out of hats. I am too big for a hat."

"No!" Lottie groaned. "You aren't listening! It isn't about you, Sofie, it's about the rabbit. I do love you, but—"

"Everything is about the rabbit," Sofie said quietly as she slipped off the bed and padded to the door with her tail trailing.

"Oh well, if you're not even going to listen to me," Lottie said in irritation. "Fine! Go on, then." And she watched angrily as Sofie went out of the room and pattered off down the stairs, her claws slipping and scrabbling, as though she wasn't concentrating on where she was putting her feet. Lottie grabbed the iPod her mum had sent her and lay on the bed, filling her mind with the music, even though she didn't hear it, just so that she couldn't feel the gap where Sofie had been.

"Lottie, dinner!" Uncle Jack was yelling from downstairs. "Danny, get off that computer, dinnertime!"

Lottie got up, telling herself firmly that she was not going to give in. She was not going to let Sofie get away with this. The little dog was being horribly selfish, and Lottie wasn't going to stop trying to rescue the rabbit, even if she wouldn't help. It was going to be hard though. Lottie relied on Sofie being there. That constant comfort and reassurance — and frequent telling off — but at least before she'd always felt that Sofie was on her side.

She stalked down the stairs and marched into the kitchen, expecting to see Sofie perched at the table, her china bowl in front of her, questioning Uncle Jack about the exact recipe he had used to make the dinner and most likely telling him it was wrong. She always wanted more garlic in everything, and she persisted in calling all the ingredients by their French names, which confused him no end.

But Sofie's chair was empty.

Lottie stood in the doorway, feeling horribly cold all at once. "Where's Sofie?" she asked.

Uncle Jack turned around from the pan of pasta sauce he was stirring and gazed at her in surprise. "I thought she was with you. You went upstairs together when you came in from school, didn't you?"

"Yes, but . . ." Lottie didn't want to admit they'd argued. "She came downstairs again," she muttered. "We sort of — she was upset with me."

"I haven't seen her." Uncle Jack looked worried, and as Danny wandered in from the little office where the computer was kept, he added, "Have you seen Sofie, Dan? She's disappeared."

Danny shook his head vaguely.

Uncle Jack frowned. "It isn't like her to miss food. I hope she hasn't gone off to do anything silly. Can you call her, Lottie?"

Lottie had promised herself she wouldn't make the first move. She was right, and she knew it, and Sofie wasn't being fair. Sofie could apologize. But now she was worried, and she sent out a gentle little call, opening her mind to Sofie hopefully.

But there was nothing. Sofie was gone.

5

Panicking, Lottie ran out into the night to look for Sofie. It was November, and very dark already, and as Lottie looked wildly up and down the street, she could only see the small circles of pavement lit by the streetlamps.

Danny appeared in the doorway behind her. "Has she really gone?" he asked disbelievingly. "It's freezing out here, and you know she hates the cold. She's probably hiding in the shop somewhere."

Lottie nodded gratefully, desperate for any shred of hope. She closed her eyes and searched for Sofie's velvet warmth in the shop. Then again, and again. She could feel the tiny magical pulses of all the mice, even Henrietta, the homing mouse, a deceptive little creature who was invisible whenever she wanted to be. She could sense Selina and Sarafan, prowling around and around their pen, in case the locks had changed since they last looked. She could see Giles the hamster in her mind, running and puffing on his wheel. But Sofie wasn't there.

Lottie looked up miserably at Danny. "She isn't there. She has to be out here somewhere, but I can't find her. I can't feel her at all, Danny! She's gone!"

"OK, OK, calm down. What did you say to her, Lottie? It can't have been anything that bad."

Danny's rat, Septimus, poked his head out of Danny's hood to hear too.

"I wanted her to help me with a spell," Lottie told them, staring out into the darkness, hoping to see a little dog running along the street toward home. "Sofie didn't want to; she was jealous because I was trying to save a rabbit from that horrible pet shop by the bridge. She kept messing the spell up, and I told her off. I — I tried to show her what it would be like to have an owner who didn't love her, but she took it the wrong way and thought I meant *I* didn't love her, and I really do!"

"Lottie, Sofie knows that," Septimus said calmly. "She may be upset at the moment, but in the cold light of day she'll realize what you meant."

"I'm not worried about the cold light of day, I'm worried about her being out here now, when it's nighttime and it's actually cold!" Lottie muttered.

"Sofie is resourceful," Septimus pointed out. "Extremely so. I wouldn't put it past her to have found a nice old lady who's a soft touch for a cute little dog. Probably within about five minutes of walking out of the shop she was sitting on someone else's sofa eating someone else's sausages. Excuse me, *saucissons*. You know what she's like, Lottie. She can really work those eyes."

Lottie sniffed, and nodded. "I know. I suppose you're right. But I don't want her to have to. I want her home with me. Pandora's out there, and she knows Sofie now. What if she finds her? What if Sofie doesn't come back?"

"She will," Septimus said firmly. But he glanced quickly up at Danny as he said it, and he climbed out of Danny's hood and onto his shoulder, to be closer to him, as though he didn't like where this conversation was going.

"I might have driven her away." Lottie gulped. "Maybe forever . . . if she really thinks I don't love her anymore. She won't talk to me, Danny, I can't feel her!"

"Have you . . . umm . . . groveled?" Septimus inquired. "Sofie is very proud, Lottie. She won't want to make the first move. You might need to beg." He looked at her thoughtfully.

Lottie sighed. "You're right. I thought she was being mean, but maybe I was a bit over the top. Look, can you tell Uncle Jack I don't want any dinner? I need to go try calling her again. And I'll beg, Sep. Thanks."

Up in her room, Lottie stared out the window. Grace's Pet Shop was in a tall, thin building, and she could see over the roofs of Netherbridge, up to Netherbridge Hill. She shuddered. Hopefully Sofie wasn't up there. Lottie focused on the stars, so clear that they seemed to hang in the sky like Christmas decorations, and thought of Sofie.

Please, please, please, she begged. *I'm sorry, Sofie. I should have been nicer. I was worried about this rabbit, and I didn't think that that would make you upset. You don't need to be, honestly. I love you. You're the most special thing. You know that, you must know that. Please, Sofie, come back. . . .*

Lottie waited, gazing hopefully out at the stars. But they only glittered coldly, and there was no answering voice in her mind. Sofie wasn't there.

Since she and Sofie had discovered their magical bond, Lottie hadn't spent a night without Sofie curled at the end of her bed. Or in her bed, sometimes, if the night was cold. Sofie liked to sleep with her head on the pillow, next to Lottie's. Lottie hadn't thought she'd miss Sofie's big ears flapping in her face.

She got up the next morning miserable and lonely, and the feeling didn't go away even when she met Ruby to walk to school.

"You look awful, what's wrong?" Ruby demanded as soon as she saw her.

Lottie didn't even bother to protest. She explained what had happened, and Ruby's face fell.

"Oh, Lottie, no! You've no idea where she is?"

"I can't feel her at all. Can we not talk about it, for a bit? I don't want to." Lottie hardly spoke on the way, but at the same time she resented Ruby's answering silence. She'd told Ruby she didn't want to talk about it, but Ruby's horrified agreement just made her feel worse.

Mrs. Laurence had decided to make them all draw maps of their houses that morning, which was good, because it was something Lottie could do with half her brain, and she didn't have to talk to anyone. But it also meant she was free to think miserable thoughts.

Dad's disappeared. Who knows where he is, or if he's even really coming back, she worried to herself. Mum would rather be in a different country than be with me. Uncle Jack only has me at the shop because he has to. And now I've even driven Sofie away! What's wrong with me?

By morning recess she was so unhappy she just wanted to snap at someone, and unfortunately it was Ruby who spoke to her first.

They were sitting huddled on a bench, staring glumly at the boys playing soccer, when Ruby asked, "Lottie, I know you said you didn't want to talk about it, but have you tried looking for Sofie?"

"What sort of ridiculous question is that?" Lottie snarled. "Of course I have!"

Ruby looked hurt, but she continued. "I mean looking for her for real. Not with magic. Going out to look for her."

"She's a magical dog, so I looked for her with magic, all right? You don't understand."

Ruby shrugged. "OK, then," she muttered. "Be like that."

Lottie glared at her. "Oh, sorry. I'm the one with the lost dog. Aren't I allowed to be upset?"

Ruby glared back. "Upset yes, rude no. I was only trying to help."

"Well, don't."

"Fine, I won't!"

"Good!" Lottie snapped.

Ruby got up, and leaned down for her parting shot. "If this is how you treat your friends, Lottie, I'm not surprised Sofie left." Then she turned on her heel and stalked away.

Lottie gasped. It felt like Ruby had hit her in the stomach, and she couldn't breathe properly for a moment. Mostly because she was worried that Ruby was right. Had she driven Sofie away? As she watched Ruby stomping across the playground, hands shoved in her pockets, her face sunk into her scarf, obviously glad to get away from her, Lottie thought unhappily that she must have. And now she had just done it to her best friend too.

Lottie had her eyes fixed on the retreating figure so closely that she didn't notice someone leaning over her shoulder, until Zara whispered in her ear.

"She doesn't look very happy, Lottie. Did you have a fight?"

"Go away," Lottie muttered.

"Go awa-aaay!" Zara mimicked, and Bethany and the others giggled worshipfully.

Zara sat down on the bench next to Lottie and smiled sweetly at her. "Tell me what happened, Lottie, maybe I can help you two make it up. After all, it would be so sad if the two most unpopular girls in the class weren't friends, wouldn't it? You might start wanting to hang around with us!" She snickered.

Lottie stared at her disgustedly. "I don't even want to *see* you, let alone talk to you." It was amazing how being totally miserable made you brave, she thought. Even after the spell, I'd normally be more scared of her than this.

A tiny frown crossed Zara's face for a second. Lottie answering back was not in her plan.

"It's a good thing you've got that little rat of a dog, Lottie, since you haven't got any other friends," she hissed, upping her nastiness level a bit.

Lottie lifted her head and looked Zara full in the face, showing her teeth, rather like Sofie did when she was angry. "Don't you dare talk about her like that!" she yelled. Hardly even stopping to think, she lifted her hand and slapped Zara.

Zara stared at her in amazement, and Lottie stared back. She was quite amazed too. Zara slowly lifted one hand to her cheek, as though she was checking it was still there. "You really shouldn't have done that," she whispered.

Lottie smiled at her. There was a wonderful freedom in having done something really, really foolish. She just didn't care anymore. "Why not?" She beamed at Zara. "It felt brilliant. Maybe I should do it again."

Zara grabbed her coat and pulled her upright. "Bethany, help me!" she snapped, and together they flung Lottie back against the bench, bruising her arm.

Lottie sprang back up. Even though she couldn't feel Sofie at the moment, it was as though she was drawing on her fighting spirit. Sofie would have loved this. She would have been cheering. Lottie was almost sure she could feel her watching, just out of reach of Lottie's mind. She ran at Zara, pushing her to the ground, and sat on her. Bethany was standing there looking helpless. She and Anya made a halfhearted attempt to pull Lottie off, but neither of them wanted to get hurt, and they backed off when Lottie shoved them away.

Then Zara started to fight back. She scratched at Lottie's cheek and Lottie yelped and scrambled away.

"Lottie!" Ruby was rushing back across the playground now, and she hauled Lottie up, both of them stumbling back, staring at Zara, who was spitting and ranting on the ground, yelling at Bethany to help her up. "I can't believe you hit her!"

"Me neither," Lottie murmured.

By now Zara was up again. She shoved at Lottie furiously, Ruby shoved her back — and that was just when Anya came back with Mrs. Laurence.

"Girls! Are you fighting?" the teacher demanded in a shocked voice.

"Lottie and Ruby are picking on me, Mrs. Laurence," Zara whimpered. "Lottie pushed me over, and she hit me."

"Lottie, is this true?" Mrs. Laurence said sternly.

"Well, yes, but . . ."

"She and Ruby ganged up on me," Zara said, sniffing.

"But . . ." Lottie wondered how Mrs. Laurence managed not to see her scratched face, as she ranted on about how disappointed she was with Lottie and Ruby. She looked disbelievingly at Ruby, who shrugged.

"Zara's had *years* of practice. Just try to look sorry," she whispered.

Mrs. Laurence put them in after-school detention — which meant she would have to call Uncle Jack and Ruby's parents.

Ruby grinned as they followed the furious teacher back into school, leaving Zara gloating to her friends. "I really hope my mum's painting. She hates it when people call. Mrs. Laurence will end up apologizing to *her*."

"Won't she be upset?" Lottie asked, wondering what Uncle Jack was going to think. He knew that Zara had bullied her before, so hopefully he'd believe Lottie's side of the story.

"Oh, probably, but she'll stick up for me to Mrs. Laurence."

Certainly, when Mrs. Laurence came out of the office five minutes later, she was decidedly pink, and her eyes were snapping with anger. "Right, you two. An hour's detention after school. You can write about why fighting is never the answer to any problem."

Lottie and Ruby nodded, and tried to look apologetic. But as Mrs. Laurence strode away, Ruby put an arm around Lottie. "What did Zara say to you? I've never seen you look like that before. And when you slapped her, oh, Lottie, I wanted to cheer. It was bliss."

Lottie grinned for a minute. "It felt good too. She called Sofie a rat, and with Sofie gone, I couldn't bear it." Her voice shook. "So I hit her." Lottie sniffed, and added, wavering even more, "I just wish Sofie could have seen!"

"I'm sorry you got dragged into that," Lottie told Ruby as they walked home in the gathering dark after their detention. "Mrs. Laurence was really unfair."

Ruby grinned. "I told you that you shouldn't have let everyone forget the spell-picture you made of Zara. Mrs. Laurence has gone back to thinking she's an angel."

"Mmm. But everyone would have known it was something to do with me, and how would we explain it? Aliens?" Lottie sighed. "It's tempting though. I really don't know how Zara does it."

"Like I said, years of practice. And she has no shame and no feelings. Anyway, forget her. We don't have to see her until tomorrow, and then I can just relive you smacking her all over again. Are you going back home to do another search for Sofie?"

Lottie shook her head. "No, I can't find her by magic; I think she's hiding herself. You know what you were saying earlier, when I was horrible? About finding her the other way, actually going out and looking? I think I need to do that."

"It's getting dark," Ruby pointed out, shivering a little. "You can't go now."

Lottie shrugged. "Well, I've got to go home first and see what Uncle Jack says about the detention, but I have to do something. I can't sit around and just wait for her to come back. What if she doesn't? Or what if she does, and she thinks I didn't even try to find her?"

Ruby looked thoughtful. "Mmm. I see what you mean. Have you got a photo of her?"

Lottie blinked, surprised. "Yes, lots. You know what a show-off Sofie is, she loves having her photo taken."

"Then I think we should make LOST posters on the computer and put them up around the town. I could stick some up for you on the way home. Mum texted me to say she thinks Mrs. Laurence is a twit, and was Zara still bullying you, so I don't reckon I need to go home and grovel." She fluttered her eyelashes hopefully at Lottie. "That's if you want me, of course?"

Lottie hugged her. "You know, when you stormed off earlier on, I couldn't believe I'd just had a fight with you as well. I was sitting there thinking I'd lost everybody, even you. That's when Zara turned up — she chose just the wrong moment. That's why I hit her."

"I'm an inspiration," Ruby said happily.

6

Lottie got up early the next morning and left for school with a pile of posters and a roll of the packing tape that Uncle Jack used for wrapping orders he sent by mail. She was glad to get out of the shop without seeing her uncle. He hadn't been mad about the detention; in fact, he'd offered again to come into school to talk to Mrs. Laurence about Zara. Lottie couldn't think of anything worse. He was worried about Sofie though. All last evening, he'd been thinking of places she might be, and asking Lottie to use her bond with Sofie to search. She'd tried so many times, and each time she'd found nothing and felt more helpless. Ariadne had come around to help, and the worry in her eyes every time they found nothing had made Lottie feel sick. She didn't want to face another barrage of suggestions this morning.

Usually if she was going out early for something, she'd ask Sofie to tell Uncle Jack, she thought sadly, and left her message with Horace instead.

The grumpy old parrot eyed her posters. "Spelled all the words right, have you? Mmmm. Good girl."

Lottie blinked. Horace was never nice. Her eyes filled with tears as she unlocked the shop door. If Horace was missing an opportunity to tell her off, it probably meant he'd given up on Sofie ever coming back.

"I'm going to find her, you know," she told him, almost angrily.

"That's the spirit." Giles the hamster nodded. "Off you go, Lottie dear."

"Go get her, Lottie!" It was Fred, dancing up and down with his friend Peach in front of their cage. They twirled their tails together like ribbons on a maypole and spun around, singing, "Lottie, Lottie, Lottie!"

Lottie walked through the misty streets, taping her posters to lampposts and fences. When she saw a shop that was open, she asked them to put a poster in their window. The waiter at her and Sofie's favorite cafe was just undoing the shutters when she went past. He was horrified when she told him, and took two posters. He adored Sofie, and always gave her extra biscuits with her espresso. He told Lottie she looked hungry, and gave her a croissant. Lottie nibbled it as she walked along, wishing Sofie was there to share it — she loved croissants.

Lottie circled back around so that she would end up by the bridge to meet Ruby as usual. She'd spotted a few posters that Ruby had put up the previous evening too. She walked past the dingy little pet shop and stared in the window. She could just see the rabbit's cage. There was a small, grayish heap in one corner — the rabbit — curled up hopelessly. He looked even more unhappy than he had before. Maybe I made things worse for him too, Lottie thought miserably. Making him think someone cared, and then just disappearing. I've got to get him away. Maybe Mum would send me some money to buy him. . . . I'll try the spell again tonight. I was too worried about Sofie to try yesterday, but the rabbit doesn't know that. It isn't his fault.

That evening, Lottie went up to her room, hearing a ghostly patter of claws on the stairs in front of her, and knowing that it was only in her mind. Wishful thinking. She felt so lonely — the idea of a complex spell with no help from Sofie was terrifying. She supposed she was being silly — it wasn't as if she was fighting against someone with this spell, as she had been against Pandora only a few days before. If it went wrong, she wouldn't be trapped by a crazy enchantress who had it

81

in for her family. But somehow the thought of all that power out there, all that magic, was simply awful. What if she broke it? What if she tried to do something that wasn't allowed, and her magic simply disappeared? What if she turned herself purple?

Stop it! Lottie said to herself firmly. There was no reason it should go wrong, just because Sofie wasn't there. It would be harder, that was all. Good practice.

And anyway, she thought gloomily, she couldn't face being downstairs right now. Uncle Jack was still in a complete tizzy over Sofie, as apparently he'd spent ages last night searching for her by magic too. He hadn't found so much as a whisker, and he was flabbergasted. Lottie suspected that he wanted to get Sofie back partly because he was desperate to know how she'd managed to hide herself so cleverly.

Lottie decided she needed something to look at, rather than just staring into the darkness. Something rabbity . . . She looked around her room, frowning, then jumped up, grabbing one of the animal magazines that she'd brought with her when she first moved to her uncle's. She hadn't bothered buying them recently, not since she'd had real animals to look at — and talk to.

Eagerly she flicked through the pages; she was sure she remembered an article on rabbits. At last she found it, a page covered in photos of rabbits gazing out at her. None of them looked exactly like the rabbit in the pet shop — he was a particularly lovely shade of soft, silvery gray, Lottie realized now — but they would do. She picked the closest, a rabbit with a pretty gray coat and an endearingly pink nose, and tore the picture out. Then she sat holding it, staring into the paper eyes and hoping. . . .

Lottie became aware of a smell. Not a very bad smell, just not quite fresh. As though someone hadn't bothered to clean out the cage quite as often as they should. And food that was enough, but the same all the time. Never even a scrap of carrot or a fresh apple. And the loneliness. No one to talk to. No one even to touch.

Hello . . . she murmured quietly, still staring at the picture in her hand.

The rabbit's pink nose twitched, wrinkling the paper, and Lottie squeaked with excitement and shock. She hadn't expected that to happen. The rabbit squeaked back anxiously, and Lottie felt guilty. *I'm sorry, I didn't mean to frighten you. Do you remember me? I came to the shop before, with my friend. We were worried about you.*

The rabbit stared at her with big dark brown eyes. The eyes glimmered with fear, but with intelligence, too, Lottie was sure. Nothing like Sofie's, but even if this wasn't a rabbit that could talk, she was sure he could understand her.

Don't be scared. Please. Can you talk?

The rabbit nodded, very slightly. So slightly that Lottie almost thought she'd imagined it. *Don't you want to?* she asked.

The paper rabbit looked around. His pretty grass-and-flowers background had changed to grubby cage bedding now. *Not safe*, he muttered cautiously, then he closed his eyes and hunched his shoulders, as though he expected the sky to fall in.

But we're only talking in our heads, Lottie reminded him. *No one can hear you.*

The rabbit frowned, the brown eyes looking confused. Then he nodded slowly. *Maybe*, he agreed in a whisper. *I'm not sure.*

What's your name? Lottie asked. *Do you have one?*

Barney, the rabbit whispered, still looking panicky.

Barney, I really want to get you out of that horrible shop. That would be good, wouldn't it? Lottie asked persuasively.

The rabbit nodded, his eyes suddenly brightening with hope.

If I call you, will you come? Lottie begged.

Barney blinked. *How?* he asked, honestly bewildered.

Lottie looked at him helplessly. *I'm not quite sure*, she admitted. *But I think it should just work — somehow. . . .*

Barney looked at her with his head to one side and blinked thoughtfully. *Do you by any chance have a dog?* he asked.

Lottie was so surprised that she dropped the picture, and when she scrabbled to pick it up again, it was only a paper rabbit, gazing foolishly from a grassy meadow. Barney had gone.

"Oh no! What did I drop it for?" she wailed. It had been working, really working, and then she'd messed it up.

Why had Barney asked her that, of all things? Had he seen Sofie in her mind somehow? Lottie supposed that anyone she tried to speak in thoughts with at the moment would be able to tell that Lottie had lost Sofie and desperately wanted her back. It must be all over her mind. She shouldn't have reacted like that.

Sunk in gloom, she lay down on the bed, staring at the ceiling and thinking of Sofie. Sofie would have caught the paper for her when she dropped it, snapped at her until she'd gotten the thought connection back, and told the rabbit to stop fussing and just come. Sofie would have had it sorted out in no time. I need her back, Lottie thought miserably. I can't do all this without her. How am I going to get her back? A tear rolled down her chin, and she brushed it away in irritation. Sofie thought crying was silly, and it was.

* * *

"Lottie! Lottie!" Uncle Jack was yelling excitedly downstairs.

"What is it?" Lottie muttered back wearily, then, realizing he couldn't hear her, she heaved herself up and went to the top of the stairs to say that she wasn't feeling well and she was going to bed.

But standing at the bottom of the stairs was Sofie.

Lottie wasn't sure afterward how she'd gotten down them. She wouldn't have been surprised if someone had told her she'd just jumped from the top step.

"Sofie, Sofie, you came back. . . ." Lottie hugged her lovingly as Sofie wiggled with delight in her arms. "I thought you weren't coming back, I thought I'd made you leave forever."

"You put posters up, with me on them," Sofie said smugly. "I saw lots of me, all over town. But Lottie, that was not my best picture. Why did you choose that one, hmm? My nose looked big. Which it is not."

"Where were you?" Lottie asked. "Were you safe? Where did you go?"

"A little girl found me — or I found her, perhaps. I slept in her playhouse, and she gave me her sandwiches. Bologna." Sofie wrinkled her nose disapprovingly.

Lottie tried hard not to look upset, but she felt terribly, terribly jealous. "Was she nice?" she murmured.

Sofie shrugged. "She was a baby. *Very* little. But sweet." She put her head to one side and looked at Lottie slyly. "When *I* was jealous, Lottie, you were angry with me. You said I was being selfish. . . ." She looked up at the ceiling, humming a little French tune to herself.

"I know, Sofie." Lottie leaned her head against the velvety wrinkles of Sofie's neck. "I've never had to share you, have I? And you have to share me a lot." She sat down on the stairs, glad that they led into the passage and not straight into the shop where the others could hear her. "But you know that I don't have the same bond with Tabitha or Giles or any of the others, don't you? Even Fred?"

Sofie pressed her nose into the crook of Lottie's elbow, hard. Her voice was a little muffled. "I know. But you love everybody so much, Lottie. And you wanted another one. . . . I am a jealous dog." Sofie took a deep breath. "I am sorry," she said, rather grandly.

"I didn't want him for my own, Sofie, only for him not to be in that shop anymore," Lottie promised.

"Yes, it is not a good place. Nobody should have to live there." Sofie shook her head disgustedly. "The smell!"

"Exactly, and no one ever talked to him, he was so— Sofie, how do you know? Did you go there?" Lottie held her out, looking at her in surprise, and Sofie wiggled expertly out of her grip.

"You had better come," she called over her shoulder, prancing into the shop.

Sitting on the counter, staring dazedly at a beautiful selection of vegetables — clearly Uncle Jack had raided the fridge — was Barney the rabbit!

Lottie gazed at him in amazement, and then looked down at Sofie. "Did you bring him?"

Sofie shrugged. "You wanted him, so I went and got him." She yawned, but she was watching Lottie out of one eye all the time.

"How?" Lottie gasped.

Sofie scrambled onto the windowsill, then up to the stool, so she could put her paws on the counter and hold court. "When I first went out of the shop, I did not mean to go anywhere in particular. I was upset and I wanted to run, that was all."

"I'm sorry," Lottie whispered, stroking her guiltily.

"It was that little dream girl you showed me, Lottie. It was all so real. I could not help thinking that that was what you really wanted, for me to live with someone else. I spent the night in the playhouse, the nice little girl's playhouse, thinking perhaps I would have to find another home. And the next day, she had to go to school, but she came back and fed me biscuits, so

I thought I might stay, even though the playhouse was cold. But then in the morning, I saw the pictures, and I knew you wanted me back. I could smell you on them, and you smelled sad. So I thought I had better make you happy again. I had perhaps been a *leetle* bit selfish. So I brought you the rabbit."

"She said I had to come," Barney the rabbit put in, a piece of lettuce trailing rather foolishly from his mouth.

Sofie glared at him. "And you made a great fuss! You cannot have wanted to stay in that place. You should have just come at once, without all the silliness."

Barney stared at her, blinking nervously. He was clearly not a rabbit of very great brain. He nodded. "Yes, Sofie," he murmured politely.

Sofie frowned. "Mmm. Very well, then."

"I still don't understand how you did it," Lottie said, pulling another stool up to the counter. "Was that horrible old woman there?"

"She went to the back of the shop to have her lunch," Sofie explained. "I could smell her nasty sandwiches. So while she was gone I sneaked in and tried to persuade this silly thing to go with me. But he just kept blinking at me, and saying he would not dare. He is a big coward!"

Barney nodded sadly. "Rabbits are," he agreed.

Sofie made an indescribable noise, something like *pffft*. It was a fairly clear opinion of rabbits. "Then the old *harpy*, she came back while I was still trying to get this fat carrot-muncher to move."

"What did you do?" Lottie asked, enthralled.

Sofie shifted her paws, as though she were rather embarrassed. "I pretended to be one of the model dogs," she admitted.

Lottie stared at her, and then giggled. "What, those horrible plastic ones in the shop? The ones modeling the leashes and those awful dog coats?"

"I sat in one of the baskets for sale." Sofie nodded. "I am unnaturally perfect, after all. She thought I was plastic." She twisted her neck and shuddered. "But I had to stay still for a very long time. My neck is still stiff." Then she frowned at Barney. "Who knows how long I would have had to be there, but then, Lottie, you told this rabbit to come."

Barney nodded. "You spoke to me," he agreed proudly. "I spoke back."

Sofie rolled her eyes. "*Sacré bleu,*" she muttered.

"So . . . when I called, Sofie was already there?" Lottie worked out.

"Of course." Sofie nodded. "And when the old woman went out to make tea, I opened his cage — the simplest catch you can imagine, why he had not done it himself, I do not know — and I made him follow me here."

"Didn't anyone notice you?" Uncle Jack asked faintly. "A dog and a rabbit, running down the street?"

Sofie wrinkled her nose. "A few people may have," she admitted. "But it was getting dark." She sighed. "And we did a lot of hiding. Rabbits, as I said, are not brave."

"Afraid not," Barney agreed, his whiskers shivering.

"We'd better find somewhere for you to sleep," Uncle Jack said thoughtfully. "Do you like to sleep in hay? I think we've got some in the storeroom. Or perhaps a cardboard box, with an old towel in it? In one of the bigger cages?"

"A box . . . ," Barney agreed blissfully.

Sofie looked expressively at her velvet cushion. "A box . . ." She shook her head. "Lottie, I am hungry. I have only had a bologna sandwich since I left. And a very small biscuit. Or two. And a toffee that someone had left in the playhouse. It was furry, Lottie, but I was *starved.* . . . And I have had no coffee at all." She held up a paw, and it did seem to be shaking. "I *need* coffee, you see?"

Barney was sitting by the open door of his cage when Lottie and Sofie came down the next morning. He was watching the shop with an air of interested wonder, his nose twitching with happiness. His gray fur had the most wonderful sheen to it — as though he were actually several different shades, depending on which way you looked at him.

"Hello, Barney." Lottie tickled him behind the ears. "Did you sleep well?"

"Oh yes, thank you." He looked up at her with concern. "But did you know, my cage is open."

Sofie stared at him. "Of course we know! We are looking at you! Your nose is sticking out of it!"

Barney jumped back apologetically, his whiskers trembling.

"It's OK, Barney. We don't usually lock the cages," Lottie explained. "When the shop's open we try and make sure they look closed, for when people come in, that's all. You can come out of the cage now if you want."

"Out?" Barney murmured, as though he didn't quite understand the concept.

"Rabbits." Sofie shook her head. "He does not have two brain cells to rub together, Lottie. Do not overtax him," she whispered.

Already Fred and Peach, who shared a cage with the other pink mice a couple of shelves above Barney's, were watching him with interest — Fred hanging upside down to spy, while Peach held on to his tail. Lottie frowned at them. She had a feeling they were going to try and dive-bomb past his cage, and the poor thing would probably have a heart attack. Fred tried very hard to look innocent, as though he was just exercising perhaps, and Peach hauled him up rather quickly.

Lottie smiled reassuringly at Barney, and she and Sofie went to grab some breakfast. "I don't think rabbits are actually dim," Lottie said thoughtfully.

"That one is," Sofie stated flatly, sniffing the cereal boxes. "No. They are all cardboard, these things. I want toast."

"He might just be nervous," Lottie argued.

Sofie raised her eyebrows.

"Well, all right, maybe he isn't the brightest bunny ever, but he's very sweet."

Sofie sniffed. "He is a fluffy *imbécile*."

"But you call me that, too, all the time," Lottie pointed out. "Not fluffy, obviously."

Sofie smiled at her, showing very white teeth. "I do," she agreed. Lottie wasn't entirely sure what she meant by that, but she suspected she was being insulted. It was nice that things were back to normal.

Lottie bounded out of the shop that morning to meet Ruby. She was desperate to tell her that Sofie was back, and also that her posters had been a vital part of bringing the little dog home, though not in the way they had expected.

She danced onto the bridge, and Ruby noticed her changed mood at once. "Is she back?" she cried. "Did someone find her and bring her back to you?"

Lottie shook her head. "No. She brought herself back. But she saw the posters, and she loved them. I think she might have stayed away longer if she hadn't had proof I was missing her. So thank you!"

School was so different with that wonderful feeling of closeness with her familiar back again — even if all Sofie did that day was sleep, claiming to be worn out by her adventures. Lottie wasn't sure how Sofie had managed to disappear so completely that she couldn't even sense her. She'd tried asking, but Sofie didn't seem to be able to explain. Lottie was just so glad to have her back, she didn't push the question. At some point she'd talk to Ariadne about it, but right now it felt like a missing piece of her had been slotted back in, and she was whole again. Or almost whole.

Every so often Lottie missed her mother badly, and since her dream on Monday night, she hadn't been able to stop thinking about her. What with the rabbit to worry about, and then Sofie going missing, her mind had felt as if it were about to burst. Now that she could think more clearly, she could see why her mother had kept coming into her mind.

What was she going to tell her? And how? She couldn't call her up and say that her father was alive. Her mother wouldn't believe her, and even if she did, it would be a very cruel thing to do. Lottie needed to be with her, holding her. But should she even tell her now anyway? What if the dream had been wrong? What if it was just a dream after all?

Lottie nibbled her pen and tried to look as though she was thinking about the story she was supposed to be writing. She scribbled another couple of sentences, to distract Mrs. Laurence.

There was only one thing to do. She needed to see her mother. Mum had been promising to bring her to Paris soon. Maybe they could talk there. Lottie wished she knew how much time they had before her father came — if he was even coming. . . .

Ruby had to go out with her mother after school, so Lottie walked home alone, still tangling with the problem of her parents. She felt as though she wasn't old enough for all this — as though these were grown-up questions. How to reintroduce your dead father to your mother wasn't something eleven-year-olds usually had to think about. She knew her mum had missed him desperately, but he'd been gone for seven years. Did she still love him, even? Lottie sighed.

Be happy, Lottie! Sofie's voice sang in her mind, with such an air of excitement and secrets that Lottie quickened her pace at once.

Sofie? What have you been doing? What's going on?

Come home and see! Sofie told her gleefully.

Arrivals, Sofie's mind seemed to be saying, and Lottie gulped. Was her father here already? Had her dream come true so soon? Lottie broke into a run, her heart thumping. She was excited and terrified at the same time.

She flung open the door of the shop and squeaked with joy. Standing there, cuddling Barney the rabbit, who was lying on his back with his paws in the air looking happier than Lottie had ever seen him, was her mother.

7

Actually, Lottie realized, after she'd delightedly hugged her mother for at least ten minutes, she wasn't just holding a rabbit. She was cuddling an *animal*. Lottie's mum didn't do animals. She'd always resisted Lottie's pleas for a pet by pointing out that she was at work all day, and Lottie was at school, and then after-school club. The poor creature would be lonely. Lottie had tried to argue for a hamster, as they slept in the daytime anyway, or even a fish, but her mum hadn't budged.

So why was she now crooning sweet nothings to Barney while she tickled his tummy like an expert rabbit handler?

Sofie frowned at her. *I like your mother, Lottie, even though she is strange. But it is very boring not being able to talk while she is here. And she seems rather too fond of rabbits.*

Lottie gave Sofie an apologetic look. *Why is she strange?* she asked curiously. Lottie had always thought of her mum as incredibly, relentlessly normal. It was why she couldn't hear the animals in the shop — because she simply didn't believe that unusual things could happen to her.

Well, she could hear us if she wanted to, Sofie told her. She didn't sound as though she was arguing. Her voice in Lottie's mind was completely matter-of-fact. She knew she was right — even more so than usual.

You mean she doesn't see what's going on here on purpose? Lottie blinked at Sofie, completely confused. *Why?*

Sofie looked at Lottie's mother, with her head to one side and a smidge of tongue sticking out. It was something she did when she was really concentrating.

Perhaps it is easier that way? she asked thoughtfully. *Or maybe she is scared.*

Scared of what? Lottie bit her bottom lip in concern.

Of what she might have to be if she could see what is real, Sofie said very slowly. *I think. But it is hard to tell. It is bad manners to snoop around in someone's mind. And there is a very thick fog in her head. She is not doing any of these things on purpose, Lottie. It is just the way her mind works.*

"Lottie!"

Lottie jumped, and her mum laughed. "You really were away with the fairies. Were you thinking about school?"

"Mmm . . ." Lottie smiled. That was typical of Mum. She considered saying, "Not quite; I was talking to the dog," but it didn't seem the right time.

"Your uncle Jack says I can have the room next to yours again, Lottie," Mum explained. "Want to come and help me unpack? I brought you a couple of things," she added persuasively.

Chocolate? Sofie's ears pricked up a little.

Lottie's mum headed for the stairs, still cradling Barney in one arm, and with her travel bag in the other.

"Mum? Are you taking Barney upstairs?" Lottie couldn't help asking.

Her mother looked down and laughed, sounding a little embarrassed. "Oh, I forgot I was holding him. He's so cuddly, isn't he? He reminds me of Alfie, the rabbit I had when I was your age, Lottie. He was a darling, just like this lovely bunny." She looked thoughtful. "Is Barney house-trained, Jack? *Could* we take him upstairs?"

Uncle Jack looked amused, and Barney blinked at him hopefully.

I think I am, he murmured vaguely in their heads.

"I'm sure he'll be fine." Uncle Jack raised his eyebrows at Lottie, who made an *I have no idea!* face back.

Her mum, wanting to take an animal up to her bedroom? Her mum, who was always saying pets were unhygienic? Lottie followed her slowly up the stairs, Sofie padding along behind.

Lottie's mum turned as she heard Sofie's claws on the wooden treads. "Oh, Lottie, I've just thought. You don't think Sofie will chase poor Barney, do you? I know she's only little, but dachshunds can be quite snappy."

Lottie stifled a laugh at Sofie's outraged face. Her whiskers were vibrating with horror. "She really won't," she promised her mum, and then she crossed all her fingers behind her back, telegraphed a heartfelt mental apology to Sofie, and told her mum, "Sofie's very well trained."

Sofie held back a growl, letting out just the faintest breath of it, to show Lottie how insulted she was.

She doesn't mean to be rude, Lottie pleaded.

I would like to sweep away that fog from her mind, just so that I can tell her exactly how rude she is being! Sofie snarled. *Snappy! What does she think I am, a Yorkshire terrier?*

Lottie loyally didn't remind Sofie about the various times she'd bitten people, and that she and Uncle Jack had to have a strict no-biting agreement. She was fairly sure Sofie only bit people when it was absolutely necessary. Even if Sofie's views on the subject weren't necessarily the same as everyone else's.

In Lottie's mum's room, Sofie sat disapprovingly on the armchair and watched while Barney wandered around investigating. Lottie's mum unpacked her bag, bringing out a beautiful sweater for Lottie.

No chocolate? Sofie asked wistfully, leaning forward on the armchair to sniff the bag. *Though that is a very chic sweater, Lottie.*

"Lots of girls in Paris seem to be wearing sweaters like that," her mum was saying. "Oh, I have missed you, Lottie. I see all the children going to school in the morning, and it makes me think of you so much."

Lottie leaned up against her. "Me too. I mean, I miss you too." She hesitated, hopefully. "Are you — are you staying for long?" Really, she wanted to ask if her mum was coming back soon, but she didn't want to hear her say no.

Her mum frowned. "I'd like to, Lottie, I really would, but I have to go back on Sunday night." She hugged Lottie tightly. "I'm sorry."

"It's OK," Lottie lied. "I can't believe you just turned up. Did you tell Uncle Jack you were coming?"

Her mum smiled. "Yesterday. But I wanted it to be a surprise for you. Did you like it?"

"I love it," Lottie told her, and for once, she didn't feel like she was bending the truth, or trying not to hurt someone's feelings, or holding anything back.

At dinner, Lottie's mum managed not to look disapproving about Sofie eating at the table. She even let Barney sit on her lap, and fed him bits of her salad, while everyone else pretended not to notice.

"So, Isobel, I didn't know you liked rabbits?" Uncle Jack asked, watching a small pink nose appear hopefully at the edge of Lottie's mum's plate, in search of tomatoes.

"I had a rabbit called Alfie when I was younger," Lottie's mum explained. "I was telling Lottie. He had a cage for when I was at school, but most of the time he just wandered around the house. He was great company."

"*You* had a free-range rabbit?" Lottie asked, pasta dripping off her fork as she gazed at her mother in amazement.

Her mum looked a little shamefaced. "He was very tidy," she assured Lottie.

"But you always said pets were no good indoors! You wouldn't let me have a hamster because you said they smell!" Lottie lowered her voice here, in case Giles was listening. His sense of tact was not strong, and

Lottie didn't think that even her firmly disbelieving mother could manage to not hear Giles if he started giving her a lecture on good manners and hamster hygiene. Particularly if he used his booming, outdoor voice.

"I know." Her mum sighed sadly. "I was probably wrong, Lottie. I'm sorry. Seeing you here, with all these lovely animals, I realize it wasn't fair not to let you have a pet. We'll have to think about it carefully when we're back in the apartment."

Lottie glanced at her. *When*, not *if*.

Sofie was staring at Lottie with huge, troubled black eyes.

Don't worry, Lottie told her. *I'm not leaving you behind, whatever she says. And I shouldn't think it'll be for ages anyway. Mum hasn't mentioned the Paris job finishing.*

Sofie gave the tiniest nod, looking at Lottie's mum. She didn't finish her pasta.

"Dad, I meant to ask," Danny put in. "What were you doing in Broadford at lunchtime? Was it a delivery? I waved, but you didn't see me."

Broadford was the next town, a bit bigger than Netherbridge, and the middle school was there.

Uncle Jack blinked. "Broadford? No, I was here all day. I knew Isobel was coming and she'd need me to pick her up at the station here."

103

Danny looked confused. He looked over his shoulder at Septimus, who was sitting in his hood again (Lottie's mum hadn't noticed this, thankfully. Lottie was sure she'd be a bit funny about rats). Lottie saw Septimus nod. "It looked exactly like you, Dad," Danny went on. He grinned suddenly. "Were you buying my birthday present?"

From Uncle Jack's sudden expression of panic, Lottie was convinced he'd forgotten Danny's birthday entirely. He even made a discreet note on the back of his hand in pen.

Danny was looking anxious now. "Did you see that magazine I left out for you to find?" he asked. "I circled the games I wanted. You did get the right ones, didn't you, Dad? I don't want another one about pink and purple ponies, *please*. . . ."

"I thought that game looked rather nice," his father muttered huffily. "I will find the magazine, Daniel. But it wasn't me in Broadford. Ask your aunt. I was picking her up at lunchtime."

Lottie's mum nodded. "He really was, Danny."

Danny frowned. "Wow. I could have sworn it was you, Dad. Although you did have a funny yellow jacket on. Weird."

The back door clicked open, and Ariadne came in, frowning. She did a double take when she saw

Uncle Jack, her frown deepening. "Jack, the strangest thing — oh, hello, Isobel, how nice to see you! — Jack, I've just seen you — or someone so like you I would have sworn it was you — walking down the road to Netherbridge Hill. I called after you, but you just didn't seem to hear. And then you slipped out of sight, and there was a . . ." She trailed off, raising her hand to her mouth and biting her fingertips nervously, as though she'd meant to say something and thought better of it.

Lottie watched her, her heart racing so hard she felt dizzy. She was almost sure that Ariadne wanted to say that there had been a unicorn.

Lottie and her mum took Sofie for a walk the next morning. Ruby was coming for lunch at the shop later, which felt strange, because Lottie knew her so well now that it seemed as though Mum ought to have met her before.

"Have we got time to go and get a coffee and some cake at that nice cafe?" Mum asked. "I know it's chilly, but we could sit outside with Sofie, couldn't we?" She reached down to stroke Sofie's head. "She can have an espresso. That's her favorite, isn't it?"

Sofie stopped dead and stared up at her in amazement, and Lottie's mum stared back. "Goodness, she

really is a caffeine addict, Lottie. She definitely understood what I just said."

"She understands a lot," Lottie told her, trying not to
laugh.

They sat outside, wiggling on the chilly metal chairs
as they waited for the drinks to come. Sofie sat on
Lottie's lap, but she graciously allowed Lottie's mum to
stroke her ears.

"She seems different, Lottie," Sofie whispered, when
Lottie's mother had gone to the restroom.

"I know," Lottie murmured back. "I think it's Barney.
She must have really loved that rabbit she had when
she was little, Sofie, and Barney's brought it all back to
her. I couldn't believe her feeding him lettuce under
the table last night! She was like — well, she was like
me!" Lottie looked hopefully at Sofie. "Do you think
maybe she's starting to open up a bit? I might be able
to tell her about you. . . ." She stroked Sofie's head
lovingly.

"It is a good thing that rabbits don't like chocolate,"
Sofie said, with a slightly anxious look. "Or it might be
difficult."

"Can you imagine Barney drinking coffee?" Lottie
giggled. They were laughing about this when
Lottie looked up and saw her mother standing in the
doorway of the cafe, gripping the door frame as though

she was frightened everything might fall apart if she let go.

Lottie half stood up, clutching Sofie to her, and then she realized that her mother was staring at something in the distance. Lottie turned to see, and gasped.

Just turning the corner of the road was someone that Lottie would have been prepared to swear was Uncle Jack. Except that she knew Uncle Jack was making flea treatments that morning, because he'd banned everyone from the workroom. And so that man had to be her father.

"Get her, Lottie," Sofie snapped. There was no one to hear but Lottie's mum, and she was in a world of her own. "Before she falls."

Lottie sprang up to lead her mum back to her chair, pushing her into it, even though her mum's legs didn't seem to want to bend. Lottie kept hold of her hand, and Sofie jumped from the spare chair onto Lottie's mum's lap. She looked down, vaguely surprised, but she laid her other hand on the little dog's back and mechanically stroked it. Lottie watched, pleased. She knew how comforting Sofie could be when she put her mind to it.

"What happened?" she asked gently. She knew what had happened, of course, but her mum didn't realize that.

"Your father," her mum murmured. "I thought I just saw your father, walking down the road. He didn't see me. He walked away from me." The coffee had arrived while her mum was gone, so Lottie guided her cup to her mouth. Anything to distract her, to bring her out of this fixed trance. Her mum sipped quietly, and the far-away look slipped out of her eyes. She was still white, but she was herself again.

"I'm sorry, Lottie. It was just such a shock. Of course, it wasn't really your father, but it looked so like him. And here, of all places. Did you see him?"

Lottie shook her head. "Only the back of someone," she said, although even then it had been clear who it was. What should she say? Lottie just didn't feel brave enough to break the news. Not when the merest glimpse of someone her mother didn't even think was him could do this to her. How could she tell her that he was really alive — that he'd been living away from her all this time? "It looked a bit like Uncle Jack."

Her mother took a deep drink of her coffee, shivering slightly. "Being here, Lottie, it brings it all back. And you're so like him. You look like him, of course, more every year, but you're like him in other ways too. Seeing you here at the shop — he loved living there, too, you know. He and Jack were so close, and then there were the animals, he was so good with them, any sort of creature. You're the same." She smiled sadly. "I just couldn't carry on here, after he went. Everyone missed him, not only me. You kept asking where he was, and when he was coming home. Every day I had to see Jack, who was so like him. Sometimes I'd walk into a room and see Jack, and think it was Tom, and I'd be so happy, so grateful that he was back. And then it would hit me that it wasn't him. It was as though he died a little more every time." She sipped the coffee again, gazing down the street where Lottie's dad had disappeared. "I'm sorry, it must have been really frightening when I reacted like that just now. But it was like losing him all over again."

"I thought you were going to faint," Lottie told her.

Her mum smiled. "I thought I was too."

"You still miss him, don't you?" Lottie asked tentatively. "It's been a long time."

Her mum sighed. "Well, it hasn't changed since he disappeared. I mean, it's like a cut's healed over, but it's still there hurting. I don't think I'll ever stop missing him." She smiled at Lottie. "This is our place for serious talks, isn't it? When we were here last time, you wanted to know all about your dad, and why I wouldn't talk about him. Lottie, I can be furious with him for going off on that stupid trip and still love him to pieces at the same time, you know." She sighed. "It's actually quite nice to talk about him. I should have told you more about him before."

"Are you — are you sure he's dead?" Lottie asked suddenly. She was testing the water.

"Oh, Lottie," her mum sighed. "Have you been hoping all this time? I'm sorry, Lottie love, but he has to be. It's been so long. I wondered, for the first year or so — it made me even angrier, not knowing. . . . He wouldn't have just left us, Lottie. I know I said he wasn't a sensible sort of person, but he wouldn't do that." She stroked Lottie's hair. "He loved you so much, Lottie. He'd never have abandoned you."

But he did, Lottie wanted to scream. She'd been wondering about this ever since she'd realized who the unicorn who'd saved her from Pandora really was. Why had he stayed away so long? How could he leave her mother with grief that was like an unhealed wound, and his little girl, Lottie, without a father?

8

Lottie was sure that she saw her father again on Sunday, just as her mum was gathering her things together to go to the station. A tall, dark-haired man looked into the shopwindow, just for a second, and then passed on. Lottie froze, staring after him, but no one else had noticed. He seemed to be getting closer and closer, Lottie thought, digging her fingernails into her palms. It was an odd feeling, to want something so badly and be so terrified at the same time. What was he waiting for? Was he going to turn up before her mother left, or not? Lottie wasn't even sure which to hope for.

Uncle Jack was going to drop Lottie and her mum at the station, leaving them to say good-bye, and then Lottie would walk back. It wasn't all that far, and she'd have Sofie for company. Her mum had been doubtful, but Lottie promised her that Sofie was very good protection, and Sofie had demonstrated all her teeth in a wolfish smile. Lottie was sure her mum didn't realize how much she went around alone in Netherbridge. She would be horrified if she knew about everything Lottie had been doing over the last few months.

They walked into the station together, and her mum sighed. "Oh, look, the train's late." She glanced around for a seat. "Let's sit over here, Lottie. I'm glad, actually; I want to talk to you."

Lottie blinked worriedly. They'd talked a lot this weekend, hadn't they? What more did her mum need to say, without anyone else around?

I do not like the sound of this, Sofie muttered in her mind.

Me neither. Lottie rubbed her comfortingly behind her ears, but the muscles were tense under Sofie's soft black fur.

Lottie's mum fussed with her bag for a moment, then looked up, very firmly letting go of the zipper she'd been fiddling with. "Lottie, I've been thinking this weekend. I really hate being so far away from you." She reached for the zipper again, but stopped herself. "I went to Paris because I was worried about losing my job, and I hated the idea of not having enough money to look after you. I never wanted you to miss out because you'd lost your dad — I mean, how could I let you lose out twice over? But what you said yesterday, about whether I was sure he was really dead . . . And I've never really talked to you about him." Lottie's mum took a deep breath. "I think we need to spend more time together, Lottie. I'm going to tell work that I have to move back here from Paris. If they don't like it and I lose my job, then that's just going to have to be the way it is. I know I can find something else, but it might not be as well paid, that's all. We might have to go without a few things." She looked at Lottie, and Lottie realized with horror that her mum was scared. She was frightened Lottie was going to throw a fit about no more iPods and pretty French sweaters.

"That doesn't m-matter," Lottie stammered. The awful thing was, a few months ago, she would have been delighted about this. She'd been begging her mum not to go to Paris and abandon her. Lottie hadn't spoken to her for two days before she left, because she was so angry. Now she'd gotten exactly what she wanted — a mum who finally understood that Lottie cared more about time with her than she did about having money for *stuff.* It was just that she didn't want that anymore. Or rather, she did, but she wanted a dad as well. And a dog. And a shop full of talking animals.

How exactly did she explain that one?

Lottie.

Lottie flinched from Sofie's voice in her mind. She didn't know what to say to her right now. She'd promised Sofie that if this happened, she wouldn't let her

mum take her away from the shop, and more important, from Sofie. But what was she going to say? Her
mum would be incredibly hurt if she said she'd rather
stay with Uncle Jack and Danny, especially when she'd
just made such a hard decision. Lottie couldn't tell her
about the shop, and even though Mum knew she loved
Sofie, she had no idea what their relationship really
was. Lottie couldn't explain that Sofie actually knew
her better than her mum would ever be able to.

I'll work something out, I promise, she told Sofie, trying
to sound reassuring.

LOTTIE!

What?

Sofie sounded exasperated. *That rabbit is here! Look!*

Lottie's mum's fiddling with the zipper on her bag
had left it half open, and a creamy pink nose was whif-
fling cautiously out of the gap. Barney got one soft gray
ear and one dark eye above the zipper and gave Lottie
an apologetic sideways look.

Lottie giggled, glad to break the tension. "Mum . . ."

"What is it?" her mum asked anxiously.

"Barney's in your bag. You know, if you try to smug-
gle him onto the Eurostar, you could be in big
trouble. . . ." Lottie put on a mock scolding face.

Her mum's worried expression dissolved. "Oh,
Barney . . . what are you doing here?"

Barney scrambled out of the bag completely and snuggled into her lap with the most ridiculous expression of rabbity smugness.

"Poor baby, I can't take you with me," Lottie's mum murmured. "Well, not right now anyway. I wonder if we could have a rabbit in the apartment — he's so good. . . ."

The loudspeaker crackled and announced that the train was now arriving, and Lottie's mum looked flustered. "Can you manage taking Barney back to the shop as well as Sofie?" she asked. "I could call Jack and get him to pick you up."

Lottie shook her head. "It's fine. Look, Barney can fit in my bag."

But I wanted her to take me! Barney protested, as Lottie tried to squish him into her shoulder bag. *She's so nice!*

Lottie sighed mentally. *I'm nice, too, and she's coming back, Barney. But she has to go on a train now. You wouldn't like it.*

Wouldn't I?

No, Sofie told him, her voice hard. She was very upset. *Big, loud, and scary.*

Oh. But she's coming back.

Yes, Lottie promised.

Good.

"Lottie, I'll let you know what's going on, all right? I

probably won't be able to come back at once; I'm on a month's notice in the Paris job, and they might need me to stay for all of that, I'm not sure. But it won't be that long." She smiled lovingly at Lottie. "Things will go back to the way they were, I promise."

Lottie waved her off, one arm around Sofie, who was wriggling with fury, and the other stopping Barney from climbing out of her bag.

She knew things could never go back. She didn't want them to either.

It was a cold gray Sunday afternoon, thankfully. It meant that hardly anyone saw Lottie struggling home with a furious dachshund and an overemotional rabbit.

"You did not tell her," Sofie muttered as she pattered down the street from the station. It had started to drizzle and Lottie felt like crying. "A month! I knew you would not say. In a month's time you will be gone, and I will be all alone."

"No, I won't," Lottie told her firmly.

"But you did not tell her that!" Sofie growled.

"I can't do it all at once, Sofie. She's coming back to England because of me. What am I supposed to say, 'Sorry, I don't actually want to live with you anymore'? Think about it!"

"So what are you going to do?" Sofie demanded.

Lottie shrugged. "I can't plan anything, Sofie. If that *is* my dad we keep seeing, or even if it isn't, when he actually turns up, everything's going to change again, isn't it?"

"Oh!" Sofie stopped and looked up at her. "You mean, we might live with him?"

Lottie shut her eyes, hoping she wasn't tempting fate. "Mum still loves him. Why shouldn't they live together like they used to?" She opened them again, and the sky didn't seem to have fallen in, so she went on. "They used to have the big room underneath mine. Mum told me. It's really nice." She took a deep breath. "And if they did come back here, I think I'd tell her about you all. It isn't fair that she doesn't know. I couldn't imagine telling her before this weekend, but seeing her with Barney, it made me look at her so differently. I could make her believe, I know I could."

"Would she want to?" Sofie asked quietly. "Your father never told her. He must have had a reason not to."

"That was because of Pandora! And Mum wasn't happy here before," Lottie argued. "I'm sure it's because she knew inside that everyone was hiding stuff from her."

"That isn't nice," Barney put in sadly.

Lottie jumped; she hadn't realized he was listening.

117

"Your mother will think you are just making it all up. Then she will drag you away from me because she will think you have gone crazy," Sofie said gloomily.

"We'll make her understand. I know she can. How could my dad have fallen in love with her if she was completely blind to magic? How could she have had me?" Lottie argued.

"Your father fell in love with her because she was the opposite of Pandora. He *wanted* somebody without magic," Sofie reminded her. "And you inherited *his* talent; it was nothing to do with your mother."

"Sofie, are you determined to be miserable?" Lottie asked irritably.

"I am only being realistic," Sofie muttered.

"OK, look. Put it this way. If my dad doesn't turn up, or even if he does and she doesn't believe us, and she still wants to move back to our old apartment, I will refuse to leave the shop without you. We'll just have to find somewhere to live where you can come too. She can't make me leave you behind! Come on, Sofie, if I have to, I'll put a spell on her!"

"You do not know enough," Sofie whispered, looking away.

"Uncle Jack would help, and so would Ariadne. They know we can't be split up. Sofie, please. You have to believe I won't leave you behind." Lottie crouched down beside her. "Is this still about you thinking I didn't want you anymore? I thought you understood."

"I do." Sofie looked up at her. "Most of me does. A few bits of me are not sure. That is all," she added with dignity, and she walked on, holding her head very high. "Come along, Lottie. It is cold."

Back at the shop, Lottie went to find some carrots to cheer Barney up. He was missing her mum already. She thought Sofie deserved something nice, too, so she made her some strong coffee in the coffeemaker, with twice the amount of coffee that it said on the package.

Uncle Jack had gone to see someone about blackbirds that could turn into bluebirds, apparently, and Danny was "doing his homework," i.e., playing on the computer. It was pleasantly quiet. Lottie went back through to the shop and sat by the counter with her chin in her hands. Sofie sat on the counter with her and stared at her through the steam from her bowl of coffee. It made her look like something from an old movie — the kind of thing Lottie's mum liked to watch on Sunday afternoons sometimes, with people saying emotional good-byes next to steam trains. I'm not saying good-bye to Sofie, Lottie told herself firmly. Whatever Mum says, I will make it work. I will make us all a family somehow.

She blinked. She hadn't realized so clearly before that this was what she wanted. She had a perfectly good family — she and Mum had been fine together until the Paris move. And she loved living with Uncle Jack and his crazy animal family.

But now something inside her seemed to be telling Lottie that wasn't enough anymore. All of a sudden she wanted Mummy, Daddy, Lottie, and their pet dog. Like something from a storybook.

Storybooks aren't real, Lottie's sensible self said. *That's why they're stories. No one has a perfect family like that. Not really. Even if it looks that way.*

Fred the pink mouse popped his head over the countertop. "Are you having snacks?" he asked hopefully. "Got any raisins? I'm starved, the others are all asleep." He was holding his tail in one little pink paw and twirling it eagerly.

Lottie sighed and fetched the bag of raisins from the kitchen cupboard, pouring out a small pile for Fred. The raisins were the size of buns in his tiny paws, and he nibbled blissfully.

The shop bell rang as the door clicked open, and her uncle's tall figure shambled in.

"You're back early. There's some coffee left if you want some," Lottie told him, picking up a raisin that had slipped from Fred's grasp. Then she realized that Sofie was gazing round-eyed at the figure in the doorway, and she looked up too.

"That would be nice," her father said politely.

Lottie stared wordlessly, and the strange, familiar figure stared back. He was very like Uncle Jack. So alike that if you didn't look straight at him, you could mix them up. But when she looked closely, it was obvious. How could she not have seen? He had the same yellow oilskin jacket on that he'd been wearing in her dream — the funny coat that Danny had seen.

Lottie had to swallow before she could speak. "Where have you been?" she asked at last. It was all she could think of to say.

Her father blinked, his expression troubled. "I've been — I've been away. . . ." He shook slightly, and swallowed, as though he was frightened.

"She has missed you," Sofie told Lottie's dad accusingly. "They all have. You should not have been gone so long."

He looked at Lottie, his eyes bewildered, as though he wasn't sure what he was being accused of. "I'm sorry," he murmured.

"Where were you?" Lottie asked again. "Uncle Jack said you went to the rain forest, to look for unicorns."

Her father's eyes clouded with some great effort as

121

he heard the name. "Jack. Yes. Yes, I found the uni-corns. I'm sure I did."

Lottie and Sofie exchanged worried glances, and Fred skittered across the table, looking up at him. Lottie's dad smiled wearily at the little pink mouse and whispered, "Nice color."

"Thank you." Fred beamed, and ran up his arm to stand on his shoulder. "I like being high up. You're big, aren't you? Is this a friend of yours, Lottie?"

Like most of the mice, Fred had a butterfly brain. Lottie had told him about her strange dreams of uni-corns, she was sure, but he hadn't made the connection. He had no idea who this pleasantly tall person was.

Lottie nodded. "I suppose so," she said quietly, look-ing into her father's eyes, hoping for him to smile, and scoop her up in his arms, and hug her.

He didn't. He coughed, nervously, and tried to smile.

With dawning horror, Lottie knew as he spoke what he was about to say.

"I'm sorry, I'm sure I should know, but — who are you?"

Lottie swallowed. She didn't know how to answer him. She blinked back the tears of disappointment. This was not how she'd pictured her father coming home, not at all. Trying to smile, she told him in a thin little voice, "I'm Lottie." She couldn't bear to add, "Your daughter." It was too hard to have to tell him. He should know! "Would you like that coffee, then?" she added, turning away from him and half running back into the kitchen, to have a moment to hide her tears.

Her father followed her, and watched her pouring the coffee.

"Lottie . . ." he said slowly. "I know you. Why do I know you?"

Lottie put the coffee in front of him and looked up into his eyes — exactly like her own, everyone had always said.

Her father was home, and he wanted to know her story — and his own. Where should she begin? Lottie smiled at him and took a deep, slow breath — forcing herself to keep calm, and not scream out that she was his daughter. It didn't matter, after all, if it took time for him to remember.

All that mattered was that she had a father again.

Read about how it all began!

It's purr-fectly magical!

For someone who loved animals, Grace's Pet Shop was a great place to live. Uncle Jack's attitude toward keeping animals seemed to be that every creature in the place should be as happy as possible. Lottie had been to pet shops at home (Mum occasionally gave in, but she always made Lottie promise that she wouldn't even *ask* for anything, they were just visiting) and although she loved seeing the animals, and daydreaming about owning them, sometimes it was a bit depressing. The cages were so small, and the pets seemed so bored. But not here. Lottie came downstairs on her second day at Grace's to find Uncle Jack building a mouse maze on the breakfast table out of all the china in the cupboards.

But even though she was surrounded by animals, Lottie couldn't help feeling a bit lonely. Danny was only a year older than she, but it felt like a lot more. He was nice to her when he was there, but he was hanging out with his friends most of the time, and when he wasn't out he was texting them, or on the computer that lived in the tiny office next to the kitchen at the back of the shop.

With no chance of hanging out with Danny, Lottie really missed her friends. She could borrow the computer (when Danny wasn't glued to it) to chat to her friends Rachel and Hannah from school, but they were out together a lot of the time.

"Why don't you take Sofie for a walk?" Uncle Jack suggested the next morning, seeing Lottie wander sadly into the shop after Rachel had just said she had to go because she was going ice-skating.

"Can I?" Lottie sounded surprised. "On my own?" Mum would never let her do that.

"Why not? Go for a stroll. Don't let Sofie off the leash, though. She's got no common sense about roads at all." Uncle Jack glared at Sofie as he said this, and she gave a sharp yap, almost as though she'd understood him.

"I won't! Come on, Sofie." Lottie grabbed her stylish red leash, and Sofie marched to the door with her nose in the air, and stood waiting for Lottie to clip it on, looking like a little princess.

"Look after her, won't you!" Uncle Jack called.

Lottie turned around to promise that she would, and then stopped with her mouth half open. Uncle Jack hadn't been talking to her. He was looking anxiously at

Sofie, almost as though he expected the little dog to answer. Then he caught Lottie staring at him, and laughed, a little embarrassed. "Well, Sofie knows all the walks around here. Don't let her get lost, Sofie!" This time he made it sound like a joke, but Lottie was sure he'd been perfectly serious before. She opened the shop door, looking down thoughtfully at Sofie. She *did* look like she knew exactly where she was going. After a couple of corners, Lottie was fairly sure that she was the one being taken for a walk here. Sofie walked perfectly to heel, but when Lottie tried to go the wrong way, she would stop dead and look at her accusingly. Lottie tried pulling her once, just a little, but it was amazing how a dog so small could apparently stick her paws to the ground and suddenly be made of solid lead. This was obviously a walk on Sofie's terms.

The little dachshund seemed to be giving Lottie a guided tour of the town. She had good taste too. She took Lottie through a really pretty park with a fountain and loads of grass for sunbathing on. There was a skateboarding area, too, but Sofie sniffed in disgust at that, and Lottie was inclined to agree. It was full of teenage boys messing around and doing stupid stunts. Sofie walked her in a complete circle around the fountain, so that she could appreciate the cool spray blowing on her face, then led her back through some alleyways to the main street. She stopped meaningfully outside a sidewalk cafe, with a window full of gooey, chocolaty cakes, and eyed Lottie demandingly.

Lottie was a bit surprised to find herself apologizing to a dog. "I'm sorry, Sofie, I didn't bring my purse. Another day, though, I promise. It looks great." Then she noticed that a couple of girls her age sitting outside the cafe were giving her funny looks, so she glared back and whispered, "Come on, Sofie."

They were wandering up the main street, Lottie window-shopping and mentally spending the large allowance Mum had left her with (guilt money, Lottie called it), when she heard a clock chiming four. Surprised, she checked her watch. She and Sofie had been out for nearly two hours! The time had gone so quickly.

"We ought to go, Sofie. Thank you for a lovely walk, though." Lottie quickly checked that no one was near enough to hear her talking to a dog as though it could understand. "You really cheered me up." Lottie scooped up Sofie and gave one of her black satin ears a quick kiss. Then she put her down again and looked at her worriedly. Sofie was so proud, would she mind being kissed? She did look rather shocked, and Lottie hoped she hadn't insulted her. Then Sofie lifted one lip in an odd, slightly shy grin, one that lasted about two seconds before she shook her ears briskly and waltzed off, not waiting for Lottie to catch up.

Uncle Jack didn't seem bothered that they'd been out so long. In fact, Lottie wasn't actually convinced he'd noticed. He was sitting at the counter with Horace, the elderly African gray parrot whose perch was in the window. Horace liked to spend a certain amount of time sitting with his shoulders hunched up, watching the passersby. He seemed to really like it when they thought he wasn't real — then he had the satisfaction of shooting out his neck and hissing insults at them through the window, just when they'd decided he was stuffed. But in the afternoons he tended to wander around the shop, clinging on to the tops of the cages with his massive knobbly claws and suddenly swooping his head down to inspect the inhabitants. He particularly enjoyed giving the mice heart attacks by suddenly shouting rude words at them, peering around his cruelly hooked beak and hurr-hurring as they shot into their shelters.

Today he was sitting next to Uncle Jack, thoughtfully crunching a ballpoint pen. Uncle Jack had one too; he was tapping it against his teeth. "But if four down is Paracelsus, then that doesn't fit!" he was complaining as Lottie pushed open the door.

"Learn to spell," somebody said grumpily. "Sorcery, s-o-r-c-e-r-y, not s-a-u-c-e-r-y, idiot."

Lottie looked around for Danny, but he wasn't there. It was only Uncle Jack . . . and Horace the parrot, who was giving her a *look* that suggested he thought she was an idiot too.

"Uncle Jack . . ."

"Mmm?" Uncle Jack had now folded up the paper so the crossword didn't show, and was apparently deep in the business pages. Trying to look innocent, he blinked around the edge at Lottie.

"Was Horace . . . was Horace helping with the crossword?"

Her uncle's eyebrows shot up into his curly hair. He looked at Horace in amazement. "Horace? No! No-no-no-no-no." Uncle Jack smirked around the other side of the newspaper at the parrot, who had hopped back to his perch and was watching them grimly. "I would never ask Horace for help with the crossword," Uncle Jack said solemnly. Then he leaned forward conspiratorially. "Do you know why?" he whispered.

Lottie shook her head, feeling as though she might be about to be let into some deep dark secret.

"He's completely birdbrained!" Uncle Jack fell about laughing at his own joke, and Lottie sighed. She clearly wasn't going to get a straight answer.

"Oh, your mum called for you, Lottie," Uncle Jack suddenly remembered as she headed angrily for the stairs. "Said it was important and to call her back at the office."

Lottie stopped on the bottom step, looking back worriedly. She just had a feeling that this wasn't going to be good news.

Dialing through to Paris seemed to take a very long time, but eventually she got her mum on the other end. She sounded very cheerful, determinedly cheerful, as though nothing was going to get her down.

"Lottie! How's it going, sweetheart? Uncle Jack said you were out with Sofie? Is that a new friend? That's brilliant!"

Lottie sighed. She knew she'd told her mum that Sofie was a dog, but Mum was so busy with work that she really wasn't taking in a lot of what Lottie told her.

"Mmm." It was true anyway. She *did* feel like Sofie was a friend. Was it really sad to have a dog as your current best friend? Judging by those two girls at the cafe, there wasn't a lot of choice for Lottie around here anyway.

"I've got some great news, too, Lottie!" Mum was sounding really excited.

"Mmm?" Lottie's voice was guarded. Her ideal news

would be that Mum was coming home, now. A tiny spark of hope started somewhere deep inside her, warming her. Lottie forgot about the fun she'd had with Sofie in a sudden rush of longing for home, the apartment, her school friends . . .

"They're really pleased with the work I've been doing over here, so pleased they want to extend the placement. Isn't that wonderful? It might mean that you have to change schools for the September term, but that would be all right, wouldn't it? You've already got one new friend. Does this Sofie go to the local school?"

"No," Lottie said dully, laying the phone — which was still squeaking with her mother's excitement — down on the bed. "No, she doesn't." And she got up and walked downstairs, trying not to skid on the slippery wooden treads, because she couldn't see through her tears.

"Are you sure you'll be all right?" Uncle Jack was looking at her anxiously. "I wouldn't leave you, but I need to pick up this delivery. It's quite important." He frowned. "I could ask Danny to stay with you!"

"No, you couldn't." Danny was sliding past the counter, smooth as a snake, making for the door. "Sorry, off to Ben's house. You said I could." And he was out, the shop bell jangling behind him.

"Danny!" Uncle Jack kept looking between where Danny had been standing and the door, as though he couldn't quite understand how Danny had managed it.

"It's fine," Lottie said tiredly. "You'll lock the shop door, won't you? And you're only going to be half an hour. I'll probably go and watch some TV." More than anything, she just wanted to be left alone, but Uncle Jack had been fussing over her since she'd come back down.

"Well, I'll be as quick as I can," Uncle Jack agreed reluctantly.

Lottie leaned her elbows on the counter, gazing unseeingly at her book. Sofie was curled up under her stool, and Lottie could hear her sleepy breathing. It was a peaceful, comforting noise, murmuring under the squeaks and scuffles from the other animals. Lottie was worn out from crying, and it wasn't long before she fell asleep, too, resting her chin on her arms.

She woke up suddenly, and realized that the shop was getting dark. Surely Uncle Jack had been gone for more than half an hour? Moving cautiously in the half-light, Lottie went to peer out through the back door.

No, the van was still gone. Sofie had trotted after her, and Lottie picked her up, feeling a little hurt. She'd said she didn't mind Uncle Jack going, but he'd promised to be back soon. Miserably, she felt her way along the wall to find the light switches.

Suddenly, she found herself with her nose pressed up against the white mice's cage. The mice hadn't noticed her and Sofie at all; they were far too busy. It was a little hard to see, but it looked as though they were gathered in a ring, like an audience. Two mice were in the middle, turning over and over, tangling their tails, clawing and spitting. It reminded Lottie of some boys she'd seen fighting in the playground at school, and she felt quite like their vice principal, Mrs. Dean, as she tapped on the glass. "Stop it! Hey!" The mice whirled around and stared at her in horror. "Don't be so mean!" Lottie added to the bigger of the two fighters, who was still standing on the little one's tail.

"Fighting never helped anyone, you know," she added, quoting Mrs. Dean as she went on feeling for the light switch.

"Huh! That's what you think!" said a small, squeaky sort of voice.

Lottie stopped dead. She felt Sofie grow very still in her arms, as though she'd stopped even breathing.

She turned around slowly and stared back toward the mouse cage, but the ring of mice had disappeared. Now they were doing all the things mice should be doing. Three of them were desperately running nose-to-tail on their wheel, casting panicked looks over at Lottie. She could almost hear them muttering *"Yes! Can you see? We're just running on our wheel! Do it all the time! Nothing suspicious about us! Talk? Us? Never!"* The large mouse who had been fighting was being held down and sat on by three others, all frantically nibbling at sunflower seeds and trying to look natural.

Lottie shook her head. She'd just woken up. She was tired. It was nearly dark. There were hundreds of explanations for what had just happened.

Yes, she thought, but the most obvious one is that I just had a conversation with a mouse. . . .

For more magical fun, be sure to
check out these tails of enchantment!